QUEST
FOR
ACACIA

THE COSMIC DIAMOND RAY

C.C. ADELAIDE

Quest for Acacia: The Cosmic Diamond Ray
Princess Acacia Series: Book 1
Copyright © 2023 by C.C. Adelaide

Edited by Dr. Black Bee
Cover design by Nain
Internal design by ACCL
First hardcover edition: October 2023

To Egypt and the Akashic Record Keepers,

who forever ruined my 3D reality.

Then the magic begins.

Contents

.One.
The Unicorns

1

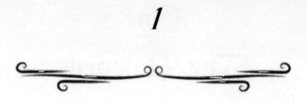

"Lily, seek the stone beneath the sea," a soft and intimate voice whispered." It holds the key to awakening Princess Acacia and restoring the unicorns' magic back to Earth."

As the little girl awoke from the dream, she felt a mysterious connection to the voice that touched her heart. It was not the first time she had dreamed of unicorns, but the first time she heard someone speaking to her.

With a sense of curiosity and wonder, she got off her bed. She walked to her window, where a golden full moon hung in the sky, casting a gentle glow upon her as if sending her a secret message through the moonlight.

"It's a full moon again," the little girl murmured, her eyes fixating on the sky's luminous orb.

Tree of Illumination

Once upon a time, a magical portal existed in a galaxy far, far away, connecting our planet Earth with a wondrous Source Light. This enchanting portal allowed magnificent beings from all corners of the universe to visit our world and share their extraordinary powers. One of these remarkable creatures was the unicorn, a majestic being believed to have come from the Lyra Constellation.

As wisdom keepers of the universe, the unicorns had a sacred duty to protect and guide their inhabited realms. Within the heart of the Lyrans' mystical land, there resided an ancient tree known as the Tree of Illumination. Its sprawling branches reached toward the heavens, glistening with the luminescence of countless stars. A magnificent crystal was nestled beneath the tree's radiant canopy, the core of the Lyrans' collective wisdom. This precious crystal also served as a gateway, seamlessly bridging the realms with the Source Light.

As the unicorns embarked on their cosmic journey, they bore the sacred responsibility of protecting the precious crystal and preserving its knowledge. Each unicorn connected profoundly to the Tree of Illumination that flowed through its core beings. When they traveled through the vast expanse, the moonlight served as a channel, connecting them with the Tree of Illumination. The unicorns would gather in a mysterious ceremony when the moon cast its soothing radiance upon them, absorbing ancient wisdom into their luminous forms.

Guided by their innate intuition, the unicorns traversed through enchanted lands, their graceful hooves leaving trails of stardust in their wake. When a rainbow arched across the sky, it was not merely a stunning spectacle; it served as a beacon, signaling the presence of a unicorn wisdom keeper. As they roamed, they sought to connect with kindred spirits and share wisdom within their ethereal forms.

The unicorns' ability to transform into different shapes allowed them to adapt to the needs of various creatures they encountered on their journeys. They would become gentle butterflies, fluttering alongside delicate hummingbirds, whispering ancient knowledge to the tiny avian companions. At times, they transformed into gentle breezes, caressing the cheeks of curious children and carrying messages of hope and inspiration.

Each unicorn possessed a unique gift the Tree of Illumination bestowed upon them. Some had the power to heal wounded hearts, mending emotional scars with a touch of their shimmering horns. Others could awaken dormant dreams, inspiring creativity and guiding aspiring artists toward their true potential. Some could communicate with the ancient spirits of the land, mediating between realms to restore balance and harmony.

Wherever a unicorn wisdom keeper wandered, joy and love radiated from them. Their mere presence could dissolve sadness and ignite the flames of pleasure within weary hearts. They carried the collective wisdom of the Lyrans, etched in the very fabric of their luminous beings. They shared it generously with all who sought their guidance.

In the quiet moments of twilight, as the unicorns gathered beneath the starlit sky, they would weave tales of ancient wisdom and secrets of the universe. Their choir of heavenly songs reverberated across the cosmos' winds, leaving an everlasting imprint upon the hearts of those who listened.

As wisdom keepers, the unicorns embraced their

role with grace and compassion. Through their radiant presence and profound teachings, they illuminated the path of enlightenment, nourishing the seeds of wisdom within every soul they touched. And as long as the Lyrans' ancient wisdom was upheld, the unicorns would continue to roam, forever guardians of knowledge and eternal beacons of love.

These amazing beings had a great love of nature and were best friends with all species, including the largest elephants and the tiniest ladybugs. With their hooves barely making a sound as they walked gently on the ground, unicorns wandered across meadows. They were a sight to behold, their pearly, dazzling coats shimmering in the dappled sunlight.

Despite being emblems of love, unicorns were open to playful mischief. Unicorns, however, continued to serve as defenders of nature's delicate balance even in their naughty moments. With a flick of their lustrous manes and a twinkle in their eyes, they would occasionally transform into other animals, seamlessly blending in with their four-legged companions. Whether they assumed the form of a mighty lion, a graceful deer, or a majestic eagle, their true nature could always be revealed by a magnificent horn spiraling gracefully from their forehead.

In their playful transformations, unicorns

delighted in exploring the world through the eyes of different creatures. They would roar with regal authority as a lion, embodying strength and courage. As deer, they would gracefully navigate the enchanted forests, their steps light and agile. And as an eagle, they would embrace the freedom of the breeze beneath the flaps of their wings as they soar through the air.

Despite their remarkable disguises, the unicorns' horns remained a telltale sign of their true nature. No matter the form they assumed, the horn retained its ethereal luminescence, casting a gentle glow that whispered of their divine essence. It symbolized their purity and grace, an unmistakable mark that set them apart from ordinary creatures.

The other animals were naturally drawn to the unicorns' presence, unaware of their appealing secret. The unicorns in disguise emanated a tranquil energy that calmed and inspired their animal companions. Harmony reigned in their midst, whether in the lion's cave, the deer's grazing area, or the eagle's lofty nest because the unicorns held within them the intrinsic wisdom and love that touched the hearts of all creatures.

Thus, the unicorns in disguise wandered the world, illuminating adventures creating harmony among various beings, and bringing up fresh ideas. They learned from each animal's strengths and vulnerabilities and, in turn, shared their wisdom, guiding others toward a deeper understanding of the interconnectedness of all living things.

These majestic horns served as antennas, allowing the unicorns to communicate with the natural world in a way only they could comprehend. The touch of their horns against shimmering crystals awakened the hidden energies within, breathing life into the very essence of the gemstones. Trees whispered their ancient secrets to the unicorns, sharing stories of the forest's ever-changing tapestry of life.

Around the unicorns, fairies, those elusive creatures of enchantment, would flit and flutter, their tinkling laughter mingling with the soft rustle of the leaves. The unicorns spoke with these creatures of magic in a language only the fey could understand, exchanging wisdom while bringing their grace to the ethereal realm.

Even mushrooms, with their humble presence, held a place in the unicorns' realm of communication. The unicorns' horns hummed softly as they leaned close to the fungi, exchanging secrets and healing energies. From the tiniest toadstool to the towering mushrooms that stood like sentinels, the unicorns understood the language of these curious organisms, their bond woven through the very threads of the forest floor.

In rare moments, when the moon's silver light bathed the land, the disguised unicorns would gather at secret groves. There, under the veil of starry night, they would shed their borrowed forms and reveal their true unicorn selves. The moonlight danced upon their horns, illuminating the clearing with an ethereal glow as they celebrated the magic within their essence.

In this enchanting ceremony, the unicorns forged a deep connection with the crystal at the tree's heart. It acted as a conduit, allowing them to share their earthly experiences and impart wisdom with their beloved unicorn kingdom. Through the resonance of their chants, their stories and insights would merge with the crystal's essence, carried across the dimensions to the waiting ears of their kin.

As the unicorns chanted beneath the moonlit sky, their voices harmonizing with the celestial energies, the crystal would shimmer and glow with radiant light. It absorbed their tales, triumphs, and tribulations, becoming a repository of shared knowledge and sacred experiences. And in exchange, as a mark of their unwavering dedication, the unicorns would receive the Source Light, divine energy that flowed through the crystal, reviving their spirits and bestowing them with renewed vigor and insight for their earthly journey.

With their beings infused with the Source Light, the unicorns would continue their sacred journey on Earth, carrying the wisdom and connection of their unicorn kingdom. Their presence became a beacon of light, fostering harmony and illuminating the path of cosmic interconnectedness for all who crossed their ethereal presence.

They were not merely mythical creatures of legend but the living embodiment of love, magic, and the intricate tapestry of life itself.

.Two.
Princess Acacia and Magicians

2

The Diamond Ray

It was said that many people and their cherished spiritual ally, the unicorn, formed a magical bond in the distant past. These ethereal beings played a crucial part in humanity's pursuit of enlightenment by acting as conduits for gathering cosmic knowledge from the furthest reaches of the galaxy. People were given significant insights through their guidance that sparked the flame of creation, developed terrific inventions, and promoted constructive change.

Once a year, the Earth portal would open wide on the eve of the Lyran New Year, connecting perfectly with the Tree of Illumination in the Lyra constellation and shining a brilliant beam of heavenly energy upon our planet for seven magnificent days. This mystical convergence marked a time of profound rejuvenation and renewal for the Earth and the unicorns who roamed its enchanting realms.

All of the unicorns on Earth gathered at this particular moment of magic, their dazzling presence uniting into a symphony of magical essence, joined in a quest to protect and revive Lady Gaia, the loving spirit of our planet.

The essence of Lady Gaia pulsed with bright vitality as the cosmic portal unlocked, illuminating the planet with the ethereal brilliance of Source Light. She was not merely a planet but a living embodiment of consciousness and interconnectedness. Her spirit resonated with the cosmic symphony, each beat echoing through the vast expanse of the galaxy.

Lady Gaia's vibrancy played a vital role in the delicate balance of the cosmos. Her magnetic fields were entangled with the cosmic energies, directing the movement of the planets and stars and sustaining life in all of its forms. She shared a profound connection with the galaxies, drawing upon their ancient wisdom and cosmic energies to maintain her vitality.

Among this majestic gathering, Princess Acacia, a rare and precious gem hailing from the farthest reaches of the galaxy, embarked on her annual visit from the Unicorn Kingdom to Earth, gracing the land with her regal presence and bringing an aura of otherworldly wonder.

Princess Acacia, a celestial being of extraordinary origins, was born from the very essence of the Unicorn Kingdom's purest diamond ray, a manifestation of sublime brilliance forged in the depths of cosmic realms. Within her being, she bore the timeless wisdom amassed through countless ages.

As she gracefully activated her horn, a wondrous transformation transpired, and brilliant diamond rays radiated forth, infusing the world with their ethereal glow. In their wake, all that was touched by these celestial beams underwent a profound purification. This revitalization harmoniously bridged the realms of Earth with the splendid source of eternal light.

Vibrant gold, silver, and iridescent blues hues were painted across the sky with a kaleidoscope of colors. The elements seemed to dance in unison, responding to the divine energy flowing through the very fabric of creation. The wind whispered with a newfound gentleness, carrying a harmonious melody that stirred the hearts of all who heard it.

Once wild and untamed, the fire burned with a serene brilliance, casting a warm, comforting glow that nurtured rather than devoured. Flames danced in intricate patterns, forming mesmerizing displays that evoked a sense of wonder and awe. Once turbulent and unpredictable, the water became tranquil and clear, reflecting the shimmering diamond rays with crystal clarity. Its currents embraced all life within its depths, carrying the essence of renewal and transformation.

The Earth, adorned with lush greenery and vibrant blooms, thrived with abundant life. From the tallest trees to the tiniest blades of grass, every living being resonated with the radiant energy of the diamond rays. Gaia, the embodiment of Mother Earth, pulsed with renewed vitality. Her landscapes transformed into breathtaking vistas, where mountains kissed the heavens and valleys embraced the meandering rivers. The very heartbeat of the Earth synchronized with the celestial symphony. This rhythmic pulse resonated with the souls of all creatures.

In this harmonious cycle, every being played a vital role. The interconnectedness of all life became evident as each entity contributed to the sustenance and well-being of others. The trees breathed life into the air, providing oxygen for all creatures. The animals roamed freely, fulfilling their part in the delicate dance of nature. The flowers bloomed and shared their fragrance, enticing bees and butterflies to carry pollen from one blossom to another, ensuring the continuation of life.

In this wondrous realm, a sense of unity prevailed. Beings of different species coexisted in perfect harmony, understanding the inherent interconnectedness that bound them together. The light of Acacia's diamond rays had awakened a deep remembrance within each soul, reminding them of their shared origins and interdependence.

Thus, Mother Earth, Lady Gaia, flowed in all her brilliant splendor beneath the gleaming diamond rays. Every part of the world felt the caring embrace of her nurturing arms, which filled it with peace, love, and abundance. It was proof of the potency of divine light and the extraordinary capacity of every living thing to jointly build a world that reflected the majestic splendor of the celestial regions.

As Acacia stood amidst this paradise, her heart

filled with gratitude and awe. She realized that her purpose transcended her journey; she was an emissary of unity and love, a bridge between the celestial and earthly realms. With each step she took, she carried the radiant legacy of the diamond rays, spreading their transformative power to all corners of the Earth.

And so, the cycle of life continued, forever intertwined and sustained by the magical connection between heaven and earth, guided by the luminous presence of Princess Acacia and the resplendent diamond rays of the Unicorn Kingdom.

The Dark Magic

One fateful day, an elderly magician named Mofa found himself venturing deep into the enchanted forest. To his astonishment, he stumbled upon the secret gathering of unicorns, including Princess Acacia. The crystal-like beauty of the princess left him spellbound, and he couldn't believe his eyes. Little did Mofa realize that unicorns were beings of pure light, and the image he saw was a reflection of his own twisted mind.

"What a mesmerizing sight!" Mofa had his eyes caught in a trance of awe and wonder on Princess

Acacia. The captivating beauty in front of him exudes an otherworldly allure that he had never encountered before in his entire life. He was taken aback by the uncommon and alluring charm she exuded in her presence.

Mofa's mind strayed into a land of greed as the magical aura of the forest swirled around. "I must acquire her," he thought, his voice tinted with ambition. He was excited and intrigued by the prospect of holding such a gorgeous being. He pondered the possible power and influence that this magnificent creature could bestow upon him.

Haunted by the allure of Princess Acacia's extraordinary powers, Mofa, consumed by his desire for immortality, embarked on a dangerous quest. He intended to capture Princess Acacia and obtain her powers of revitalization and immortality.

"Uloo, where are you?" Mofa's voice rang out urgently, every second feeling precious and fleeting.

"My lord, here I am," Uloo replied, appearing from the shadows. He was Mofa's timid and loyal servant, ready to support his master no matter the endeavor.

"Guess what! I just found out Princess Acacia wasn't merely a fairy tale; I saw her with my own eyes among her fellow unicorns in the forest," Mofa said.

"We need to create the most powerful potion to capture her." His thoughts raced as he delved deep into his vast knowledge of magic, searching for a remedy to catching the enchanted gem.

"What are the most powerful creatures in the world?" Mofa pondered aloud, looking to Uloo for direction.

The wary servant's eyes flickered with thought, and suddenly, a revelation struck him. "I've heard tales of dragons, the dominant beings in the mystical realms," Uloo suggested.

"They might hold the power we seek." A wicked grin spread across Mofa's face as he chuckled menacingly.

Together, Mofa and Uloo set out on their dark quest, driven by the allure of Princess Acacia's magic and the insatiable thirst for power that consumed them both. They delved into the darkest corners of ancient lore and the forbidden realms of dark sorcery. In addition, they sought rare and arcane ingredients, including the feathers of a mythical phoenix, a mermaid's moonlit tears, and a dragon's iridescent scales.

Yet, Mofa hungered for even more potent and sinister elements. Driven by a twisted desire for ultimate power, Mofa ventured deep into the treacherous underground catacombs. He discovered an ancient tome of forbidden spells in the depths where light dared not penetrate. From its tattered pages, he extracted a single incantation laced with pure malice and corruption.

Mofa and Uloo continued to his experiment and carefully mixed the newly discovered spell into the magic potion they had created. Its threatening presence radiated a discernible atmosphere of gloom with shadows dancing inside it. Adding this evil enchantment would ensure that Princess Acacia's transformation and power binding would endure.

As they created the component, the once timid Uloo grew increasingly uneasy. He had always been loyal to Mofa, but the darkness that now enveloped his master was palpable. He knew the danger they were diving into and questioned the wisdom of their actions. However, fear kept him silent, and he continued supporting Mofa, hoping his doubts would be unfounded.

The air grew heavy with an ominous aura as the concoction took shape. As the last drop of the potion was added, it emitted an eerie glow, signaling its dreadful potency.

"The time is near, Uloo," Mofa whispered, his eyes gleaming with malice. "With this extract, I shall possess the powers of Princess Acacia and become immortal. No one will dare stand in my way!"

Uloo's heart sank as he realized the true extent of Mofa's evil intentions. He knew that such power could only lead to destruction and chaos. The thought of betraying his master crossed his mind, but fear of retribution kept him silent.

The laboratory was enveloped in foreboding darkness as the night wore on, mirroring the malevolence that brewed within Mofa's heart. The portion was complete, and Mofa held it aloft, a wicked grin spreading across his face.

"Now, my dear Uloo, it is time for the next step," Mofa declared, his voice dripping with anticipation. "With this magic portion, we shall seek out Princess Acacia in the forest, capture her, and take her powers for ourselves!"

Mofa's heart beat faster as the final day of the galactic portal opening drew near. As they stepped into a moonlit clearing, a sight beyond imagination unfolded. The radiant presence of Princess Acacia illuminated the night, her beauty transcending mere mortal description. Surrounding her were a group of majestic unicorns, their graceful forms bathed in ethereal moonlight.

"What a gorgeous!" Mofa gasped, his eyes fixated

on Princess Acacia, his heart consumed by a desire he had never known. "I must possess her magic, for it shall make me invincible!" His mind swirled with thoughts of grandeur and domination. "Uloo, ready the extract!" Mofa commanded, his voice persistent.

Uloo hesitated, a sense of trepidation creeping into his heart. He had always been loyal but sensed the impending darkness that would befall them should they proceed. Yet, he dared not defy his master, fearing the consequences of such disobedience.

Mofa took the chance as Acacia was showered in the intergalactic energies and stood at the portal's edge. He spilled the evil mixture with a vicious grin across her defenseless form.

"Ma Yav Sza Kie Riv"

"Hear my words, oh Princess Acacia," Mofa clenched with twisted satisfaction, "As the fluid mingles with your essence, I bind you to my will, surrendering your power as darkness has taken over your soul. You are no longer a beacon of light. Your fate will be intertwined with mine."

The air crackled with eerie energy as Mofa's spell took hold, weaving its insidious tendrils around Acacia's being. A shiver ran down her spine as she felt the enchantment tighten its grip, constricting her powers and clouding her mind. The vibrant hues that once danced within her eyes dulled to a somber gray, reflecting the loss of her connection to the unicorn kingdom.

"Go back to protect the Source Light immediately," Princess Acacia commanded the unicorns swiftly the moment she was trapped in the spell's grasp. Her voice held authority despite the magical bind.

"Bang!" The unicorns around her were startled and felt a disturbance of significant size in the galaxy as a vast explosion resonated through the earth from a distance. The shockwave sent tremors trembling through the water as it shook through the air in a booming echo of raw strength. The explosion resonated in their ears, a sound that seemed to split the very fabric of the cosmos, and their strong intuition sensed the situation's urgency.

Despite their worry for Acacia's safety, the urgency of projecting the Source Light left them with no time to spare. With no hesitation, they aligned with Acacia's resolute command, their actions synchronized as they swiftly headed toward the portal of light. The weight of the situation hung in the air, propelling them forward with a determination that defied the chaos around them.

In an instant, a breathtaking metamorphosis

occurred. Princess Acacia, once a vision of grace and radiance, was encased in a shimmering crystalline cocoon. Her essence was suspended in time, her powers restrained, and she became a captivating crystal of unparalleled beauty and untapped potential.

Mofa reveled in his wicked triumph, convinced he had subdued the princess and harnessed her formidable magic for his nefarious purposes.

With a heart brimming with nefarious intent, Mofa cunningly snatched the crystal, his hands trembling with anticipation. Aware of its immense power, he knew he had to make a swift escape. With a sinister grin, he whispered dark incantations, invoking forbidden spells to manipulate the crystal's energy.

The air crackled with unsettling energy as Mofa felt the crystal respond to his malevolent touch, pulsating with an ominous glow. Clutching the crystal tightly, a wicked gleam in his eyes, Mofa hastened his pace, darting through the shadows as he made his way back to his lair, each step driven by his insidious purpose.

Mofa delved into the depths of his dark magic, determined to awaken the dormant power within the crystal. He scoured his vast collection of ancient tomes and grimoires, flipping through pages filled with arcane symbols and cryptic incantations. From sunrise to sunset, he chanted spells in hushed whispers.

Under the pale moonlight, Mofa stood in the heart of a sacred circle, surrounded by flickering candles and the lingering scent of ancient herbs. He danced and twirled, his movements an intricate weaving of spells and enchantments, as he tried to align the crystal's energy with the celestial forces above. But even the moon, with all its mystical allure, couldn't coax the crystal to awaken.

In the darkest hours of the night, Mofa retreated to a long-forgotten tomb hidden beneath his lair, the air thick with the scent of decay and forgotten souls. There, he conducted forbidden rituals, drawing upon the life essence of creatures unfortunate enough to cross his path. Animal blood stained the ground as Mofa hoped to offer a sacrifice to appease the crystal's dormant power. Yet, despite his gruesome efforts, the crystal remained stubbornly lifeless.

Driven to the brink of madness, Mofa ventured into the depths of his subconscious. Through twisted corridors of his mind, he confronted his deepest fears and desires, hoping to unlock a hidden truth that would awaken the crystal's potential. But the labyrinth of his thoughts proved treacherous, leading him down maddening paths that only further trapped his soul.

With each failed attempt, Mofa's anger transformed into a fierce obsession. He became consumed by the crystal's enigmatic allure, unable to tear his gaze away from its inert form. The lines between day and night blurred as he persisted, his eyes bloodshot and sleepless, his body a vessel driven solely by the insatiable thirst for power.

But little did Mofa know that the crystal possessed its consciousness, its own will. It waited, observing his relentless pursuit, aware of the darkness that tainted his intentions. It would not yield to his forceful demands, for its true awakening required a pure heart and a noble purpose.

"I wouldn't believe I couldn't wake you up," Mofa roared angrily as he faced the implacable crystal. His voice sounded frustrated and angry as if he had been betrayed by an entity he thought he could control.

As the days moved into weeks, and the weeks into months, the crystal's dormant energy grew restless, pulsating with an otherworldly longing. Its destiny was intricately intertwined with the forces of the universe, and only the chosen one would unlock its true potential.

In his relentless quest for power, Mofa was blind

to the whispers of the crystal's desires. The crystal would not awaken for him, no matter how dark or desperate his methods were. It patiently awaited the arrival of the one who would heed its call, someone pure of heart and unwavering in their dedication to restoring balance and harmony.

Mofa had no idea that his compulsion for the crystal would lead him down a difficult path, where his darkness would eventually consume him and imprison him in a prison of his design. Mofa's perverted aspirations would ultimately lead to his destruction because the power of the crystal could not be used by a heart filled with hatred.

His frustration consumed him, increasing his rage and pushing him to the verge of insanity. His fury grew with each failed attempt, spreading shadows of darkness across his contorted face.

Uloo, Mofa's trembling assistant, watched in silent terror from the shadows. His beady eyes widened with fear as he observed Mofa's futile endeavors. Uloo knew the consequences if Mofa's plans were thwarted or he was seen as a hindrance to his dark desires. The weight of Mofa's anger pressed upon him, a suffocating force that made it difficult to draw breath. Uloo dared not utter a word, fearing the wrath that would befall him for any perceived interference.

Mofa discovered himself falling into a maddening downward spiral as a result of his constant failures. Every bird's song and every whispered chat caused the once peaceful sounds of nature to change into mocking laughter in his ears. Each sound became a stinging reminder of his flaws, increasing his annoyance and threatening his sanity.

The black magic he had cast upon Acacia took a toll on Mofa's frail body. His once vibrant and commanding presence now withered, his skin pale and sickly. Each spell he had woven with dark intentions reflected back upon him, draining his vitality like a parasitic force. His energy waned daily, leaving him weak and trembling, a shell of his former self.

As his physical strength waned, so did his mental fortitude. Shadows danced at the periphery of his vision, taunting him with fleeting glimpses of what could have been. Illusions twisted and writhed, distorting reality, as Mofa's mind teetered on the precipice of madness. The weight of his failures bore down upon him like a heavy yoke, pressing him further into the abyss of despair.

In his secluded lair, the air grew thick with an oppressive silence, broken only by his ragged breaths and the faint echoes of his desperate pleas for redemption. He was a prisoner in his mind, tormented by the consequences of his vicious actions. Regret clawed at his conscience, tearing away the remnants of his sanity.

Nevertheless, a shred of realization poked through the turmoil of his imploding existence. Mofa saw that the crystal, his once-desired prize, had contributed to his downfall. He couldn't control its force; it slipped through his fingers like sand. He now had to deal with the fallout from his cunning aims.

Each attempt failed, and the once exquisite crystal gradually lost its shine, fading into an unappealing rock. Disappointment surrounded Mofa like a suffocating shroud, gnawing at his spirit.

As Mofa stormed out of his abode, seeking solace in the embrace of the seashore near his place, Uloo cautiously followed from a safe distance, still gripped by trepidation. Watching as Mofa's hands clenched the lifeless stone tightly. Uloo's heart skipped a beat, unsure of what further chaos his anger might unleash upon the world.

Mofa's voice echoed across the ocean's expanse, his anger and frustration palpable. "You wretched fiend, lurking within a foul and despicable stone!" he shouted like crazy, his emotions tumultuous.

With a furious motion, Mofa hurled the stone into the boundless expanse of the ocean. The water swallowed the stone with a thunderous splash, generating a resonating vibration.

"That's not good, I am doomed," Uloo murmured, his voice trembling with a mixture of awe and apprehension, as he bore witness to Mofa's furious action. The gravity of the situation weighed heavily on him, and a sense of unease settled over his already timid demeanor.

The mermaids, who lived in the ocean's depths, sensed the trembling and exchanged troubled glances as they searched for the cause of this disturbance in their tranquil realm.

Intriguing by the disturbance in their domain, graceful mermaids swam quickly toward the source of the uproar. They grabbed the rough stone from the depths with nimble hands and gently cradled it in their otherworldly embrace. The once-ugly rock shimmered and sparkled with renewed beauty as the light of their underwater world danced along its surface.

In awe of the stone's transformation, the mermaids recognized its profound enchantment. Sensing its connection to a realm beyond their own, they realized that this extraordinary stone held the key to untold mysteries and hidden powers. With reverence, they carried the revitalized stone to their magnificent underwater realm, eager to uncover the secrets it held and unlock its dormant magic.

.Three.
Unicorns
Transformation

3

The moment Princess Acacia was crystallized, she became vividly aware of her transformation's immense impact on the stability of the diamond ray and the Source itself. Quickly and selflessly, she tapped into her telepathic abilities, sending a persistent message to all the unicorns scattered across the Earth, "Go back to protect the Source Light. I'll find a way to get away."

As the message reverberated through the minds of the unicorns, a profound understanding washed over them. Each unicorn faced its own internal struggles as well. The weight of their separation from Princess Acacia bore heavily upon their hearts. They yearned for her safety and sought a way to rescue her from the clutches of Mofa's dark magic.

They realized, however, that protecting the source and the delicate balance of the worlds was more important than their presence on Earth. The unicorns left their earthly links and began their trip back to Lyra with heavy hearts but firm resolve.

The explosion caused by Acacia's transformation had created an explosive ripple effect, unsettling the cosmic equilibrium. The unicorns, guided by their innate wisdom, recognized the urgency of their mission. They embarked on a celestial voyage, their majestic forms shimmering across the night sky as they returned to their beloved Unicorn Kingdom.

United by their shared purpose, the unicorns concentrated their efforts on safeguarding the Source Light, holding it steadfastly within the boundaries of Lyra. They knew that protecting the Source was also defending the hope for Princess Acacia's eventual liberation and restoring harmony to the realms.

A profound silence fell over the Earth as the unicorns returned to their celestial world. The unicorns had not abandoned their relationship with the planet they loved. Hence their departure was only temporary. They patiently awaited the day when the forces aligned and the princess would be free again, ready to join them in their mission of love, healing, and the eternal pursuit of harmony.

Guardians of the Ocean Depths

However, amidst the unicorns' retreat to Lyra, the close guards of Princess Acacia, a select group of courageous and selfless beings, emerged from their ranks. These loyal and devoted protectors had been by her since birth, sworn to shield her from any harm that threatened to befall her. They shared a deep bond with the princess, their lives intertwined with hers in a sacred duty to ensure her safety and well-being.

When Princess Acacia issued her final orders to protect the Source Light and return to Lyra, the close guards took her words to heart. They took her directions as their compass, bearing the weight of her faith and the gravity of their mission. They set off on their quest with unwavering purpose, their hearts overflowing with love for their princess and a vow to grant her wishes.

As the close guards ventured off on their journey, they could feel the weight of Acacia's absence. Each step they took, each obstacle they overcame, only deepened their conviction that something had gone awry.

A sense of urgency gripped Acacia's close guards, the chief guard Haile, her childhood friend and close guard Cahira, and the royal Hania. Something felt amiss, and they couldn't shake the feeling of unease.

"Something went wrong. Acacia is losing her essence," Haile said with worry etched across his face.

Cahira nodded in agreement, her concern mirroring Haile's. "I feel the same," she added, her voice tinged with urgency.

"We cannot leave her behind. We must go back for her," Hania declared, his sense of duty propelling him to take swift action.

They and some other guards decided to journey back to Earth just as the portal began to close. A surge of urgency propelled them forward, urging them to reach their destination before it was too late.

Determined to uncover the truth, they traveled relentlessly, looking for evidence of Princess Acacia. Months passed as the guards traveled enormous distances, embarked into undiscovered territory, and endured many hazards in their unrelenting pursuit. Their unwavering commitment paid off when they finally met the wise fairy—a legendary figure whose ancient knowledge transcended realms and dimensions.

In the presence of the fairy's profound wisdom, the close guards eagerly sought answers about Acacia's whereabouts, their voices laced with hope and trepidation. With reverence and urgency, they implored the fairy for information about Acacia's whereabouts. Then, with heavy hearts, they learned of her crystallization and subsequent disappearance into the depths of the ocean.

With their shimmering horns and radiant presence, the close guards embarked on a dangerous quest to rescue Princess Acacia from the clutches of the crystal. Their determination was unwavering, fueled by an unbreakable oath to defend their beloved princess. Guided by their innate wisdom and intuition, they ventured through treacherous realms, navigating labyrinthine passages and overcoming formidable obstacles.

The chief guard of Acacia, Haile, stood tall amidst the shimmering, resolute ranks of his fellow guards. They were more than just a loyal retinue; they were a family bound by an unyielding dedication to their princess and a shared reverence for Lady Gaia's spirit. Their hearts filled with a profound sense of duty and determination as they gathered.

"Let us not forget our Lyran origin," Haile stated, putting the weight of their solemn mission on his shoulders. "In the depths of our souls, we also carry the essence of Lady Gaia, the very spirit that binds us to this precious planet. We will venture forth with a steadfast resolve to bring Princess Acacia back, restoring the Source Light to Earth. We shall accomplish the impossible as one."

"We are one!" the whole guards echoed Haile's words in a powerful and wholehearted chorus. "For Acacia, For Lyra, and Lady Gaia!"

Their bright bodies shimmering with throbbing energy, these courageous unicorns established a sacred circle while channeling their inner magic. An enormous wave of oneness and wisdom from the past surged through them as their horns lined up and their hooves touched the ground. They gradually closed their eyes as their combined intentions blended into a harmonious symphony.

A miraculous metamorphosis started with each breath. Their horns erupted in glistening light, engulfing their majestic figures in a bright radiance. As their ethereal bodies vanished and assimilated into existence's fabric, the air shook with expectancy. The circle of unicorns stood at the center of a mesmerizing spectacle, their forms shifting and reshaping.

Their slender frames gracefully elongated, their limbs seamlessly morphing into powerful flippers that propelled them through the depths with majestic ease. The ethereal manes that once cascaded like starlight transformed into sinewy patterns adorning their backs, mirroring the intricate beauty of the ocean's currents. Their eyes, once reflective of the heavens above, now gleamed with the secrets and mysteries concealed within the ocean's depths.

As the sacred circle dispersed, a sight never witnessed before unfolded—a magnificent "Doga" pod emerged. For the first time in history, the ocean's largest mammals appeared on Earth. The unicorn guards transformed themselves into majestic "Doga." Their arrival is an astounding testament to these extraordinary beings' unwavering determination and selfless sacrifice. The oceans and the Earth embraced them, acknowledging the profound significance of their presence and the unity they embodied.

Their presence was an enchanting revelation. Their ethereal silver-white color captivated all who beheld them, akin to moonlight dancing on the ocean's surface.

When a light shone on them, the true wonder of the Doga was revealed. Their pearlescent skin exploded into rainbow tints as the sun's rays caressed their gleaming bodies, splashing the surrounding waters in a kaleidoscope of colors. It was as if the essence of light dwelt within them, and they reflected its splendor in a dazzling display.

And, especially at full moon, illumination painted the scene in breathtaking hues. A profound transformation unfolded as the moonlight bathed the shimmering figures of the Doga. Their formerly radiant forms transitioned into a magnificent golden color, marking a transcendent change that unveiled their true nature as unicorns. Only those profoundly blessed might catch a glimpse of their unicorn light form.

Their presence brought a harmonious balance to the ocean's depths, as they swam with grace and purpose, their immense tails creating intricate patterns in the water. Wherever they went, they carried an air of mystique and wonder, inspiring those who caught a glimpse of their radiant beauty.

With each passing night, the Doga sang a hauntingly beautiful song. This melodic symphony resonated through the vast expanse of the ocean. It was said that their music carried the wisdom of the Unicorn Kingdom and the secrets of the galaxy, a celestial message of hope and unity that touched the hearts of all who listened.

The Doga plunged into the depths of the ocean with a sense of renewed purpose, their enormous bodies gracefully and powerfully negotiating the currents. The sheer size of their existence demanded reverence and awe as they broke the surface. Their immense tails created gentle ripples, weaving intricate patterns in the water, a testament to their eternal connection to the cosmos.

Within the depths of the vast ocean, they became guardians of the underwater realms, their presence offering solace and protection to the myriad creatures that called the depths their home. The Doga carried within them the ancient wisdom of the Unicorn Kingdom, their immense bodies acting as a living radar, attuned to the subtlest shifts in the cosmic energies.

Patiently, they awaited the moment when their mission would be fulfilled and when they would once again reunite with the galaxy and Princess Acacia. Their song echoed through the vast expanse of the ocean, a melodic symphony that resonated with the currents and carried the hope of a long-awaited reunion. With each harmonious note, the Doga embraced their new existence. Their colossal forms embody unwavering unity and resilience.

The Starlight Codes

With the unicorns' radiant light dimming and Earth's once-vibrant energy waning, a subtle yet profound shift began sweeping the world. Without a touch of the unicorns' purifying power, time seemed to speed up, and human age hastened. The world started to lose its shine, becoming a pale reflection of its former lively self. Nature moaned beneath the weight of the disconnect, yearning for the return of its ethereal protectors.

Little known to many, another group of unicorns, the pioneers from the unicorn kingdom, nurtured a profound affection for humanity and Lady Gaia in their hearts. This affection led them to make a committed choice: to remain on Earth. Undaunted, they dedicated themselves to their sacred duty, propelled by an unyielding resolve to safeguard the flame of hope. With bravery and tenacity, they embarked on a bold venture destined to forever alter the course of human fate.

These unicorns met in a secret grove hidden deep within the enchanted woodland under the glowing glow of a full moon, their radiant forms decked with elaborate emblems of their quest. They made an exceedingly difficult but unanimous decision to turn their essence into ethereal light codes and instill them in the DNA of humans with an unwavering love for nature and a deep connection with animals.

With a harmonious resonance, the unicorns unleashed potent energy, glistening strands of moonlight intertwining with their majestic forms. As the light enveloped them, their bodies gradually dissolved into cascades of shimmering particles, each holding a fragment of their ancient wisdom and power. These radiant particles danced in the night air, weaving a tapestry of luminescence.

Unbeknownst to the humans, scattered across the

vast expanse of the world, destiny's hand gently guided the unveiling of this grand cosmic plan. Under the cloak of night, as the moon cast its gentle glow upon the slumbering Earth, the light codes descended upon the chosen individuals, penetrating their very being at a cellular level. Embedded within their DNA, the starlit essence merged seamlessly with their human forms, forever altering their spiritual makeup.

Under the moon's watchful eye, these individuals experienced a vivid dream—a dream of a celestial dance where unicorns and humans merged in a sacred embrace. In this ethereal realm, the unicorns whispered their intentions, their hopes for a world united in love and harmony. Though the humans did not understand the intricacies of the dream, they awoke with a lingering sense of purpose and a profound longing to protect and nurture the natural world.

These starlight codes carried within them the ancient memories and profound wisdom of the golden eras when unicorns and Earth flourished in harmonious unity. They encoded the essence of purity, compassion, and the inherent magic within both unicorns and humans. As the cosmic dance of destiny unfolded, the codes patiently awaited their destined moment, dormant within the chosen individuals.

.Four.
King Orion and
Queen Seraphina

4

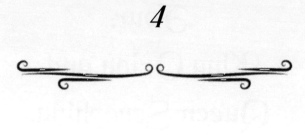

"**B**eloved wise ones, we stand at a critical juncture. Princess Acacia, our beacon of hope, has been trapped, and the connection with Earth remains severed. But together, we possess the wisdom and the light to overcome this challenge." King Orion addressed the council, his voice resonating with power and compassion.

"We must find a way to connect with those humans who carry the unicorn light code within their DNA," Queen Seraphina said, her eyes glittering with a flash of ethereal brilliance. "They hold the potential to unlock the path to Acacia's awakening and the revival of the unicorn magic on Earth."

☆

King Orion, a regal figure of noble stature, possessed a commanding presence that mirrored the brilliance of the stars. His mane, a celestial tapestry of midnight blue and shimmering stardust, cascaded down his broad shoulders, exuding an aura of cosmic grandeur. Adorned with a crown embedded with precious gems that mirrored the constellations, his majestic unicorn horn gleamed with a radiant light, illuminating the path of his subjects with unwavering clarity.

His voice carried the resonance of ancient wisdom, echoing through the hallowed halls of the Unicorn Kingdom. Under his guidance, the kingdom flourished, its magic intertwined with the harmonious rhythms of the cosmos. King Orion's strength and determined resolve made him a beacon of hope, a pillar of leadership that inspired the unicorn realm to reach for the stars and embrace their extraordinary destiny. With every stride, his noble presence commanded the respect and admiration of all who stood in his face, a true embodiment of regality and magnificence.

Queen Seraphina, the embodiment of grace and enchantment, possessed a presence that captivated all who beheld her. Her luminous unicorn horn emitted a gentle, iridescent glow, illuminating the surroundings with a kaleidoscope of colors. It was a beacon of hope, symbolizing her wisdom and connection to the cosmic energies. Her flowing mane, comprised of strands of silver interwoven with sparkling diamond dust, cascaded down her regal form, evoking a sense of ethereal beauty and celestial elegance. With each step she took, the air seemed to shimmer and dance harmoniously with her divine presence, an ethereal symphony of light and magic.

Within the majestic depths of the Unicorn Kingdom, King Orion, and Queen Seraphina ruled with grace and wisdom, their presence radiating a sense of ancient power. They were the custodians of the realm's profound knowledge, entrusted with safeguarding the ethereal diamond light that served as the nexus between their kingdom and the vast expanse of galaxies beyond.

Amidst this magnificence, the splendorous Tree of Illumination stood in the celestial dimension. This ancient tree, with its sprawling branches and luminescent leaves, served as a conduit for the Source Light, connecting the kingdom to the vast cosmic energies that permeated the universe. It stood as a bridge between the mortal and celestial realms, a sacred focal point where the magic of the unicorns and the wisdom of the cosmos intertwined.

It was beneath the shimmering canopy of the Tree of Illumination that the union between King Orion and Queen Seraphina took place in a ceremony of profound significance. As they joined their lives and destinies, their horns gently touched, creating a luminous connection that extended deep into the crystalline core of the unicorn kingdom. The union of their love infused the crystal with a powerful resonance, resonating with the frequencies of the Source Light itself.

Princess Acacia, the destined child of King Orion and Queen Seraphina, came into the world bathed in the radiant glow of the Tree of Illumination. As she emerged from her mother's embrace, a mesmerizing diamond, born from the very essence of the Source Light, adorned her forehead. This extraordinary gem, a symbol of her divine lineage, shimmered with the wisdom and purity of the cosmos.

From the moment of her birth, Acacia was embraced by the unicorns, who recognized the significance of the diamond that graced her brow. It was proof of her extraordinary destiny and connection to the Tree of Illumination and the Source Light. The diamond shone brighter than anything they had ever seen, reflecting the cosmic power and guidance she would carry throughout her life.

As Acacia grew, her bond with the Tree of Illumination deepened. She would often seek solace within its embracing branches, the diamond on her forehead resonating with the celestial energies that flowed through the tree. It whispered ancient wisdom and cosmic secrets into her ears, filling her heart with a deep understanding of the interconnectedness of all existence.

Acacia discovered her intrinsic capacity to harness the power of the diamond light within her as she matured. With focused intention and unwavering belief, she could summon the radiant energy and channel it through her horn, creating dazzling diamond rays that emanated pure love and healing vibrations.

Whenever she activated her diamond light, the surrounding space would be enveloped in a kaleidoscope of shimmering colors. The diamond rays cascaded like waterfalls, infusing everything they touched with a revitalizing essence. They danced with the wind, breathed life into the flora, and ignited a sense of wonder in all who witnessed their splendor.

Acacia's diamond light could purify and transmute negativity into positivity, gently dissolving barriers and restoring harmony. It held the secrets of cosmic creation and the potential to awaken dormant potentials in those open to its transformative touch. Acacia became known as the "Harbinger of Diamond Light," a beacon of hope and renewal in a world yearning for healing and restoration.

Princess Acacia, the embodiment of the Source Light, carried within her the legacy of the Tree of Illumination and the radiant diamond bestowed upon her at birth. Her destiny was intricately woven with the Unicorn Kingdom's fate and the cosmos' harmonious balance.

☆

Upon witnessing the mysterious disappearance of Princess Acacia and the subsequent closure of the galactic portal, King Orion and Queen Seraphina recognized the magnitude of the challenge they faced.

They called upon the wise ones from every part of the universe in a flash of great insight. Together, they summoned a grand council to pool their collective wisdom, searching for the key to restoring the severed connection between the unicorns and the inhabitants of Earth.

Whispers had reached the unicorn kingdom's ears, conveying stories of transformation and sacrifice. Some of their brethren, the majestic unicorns, had chosen to embark on a new journey, forsaking their light form to become magnificent Doga, guardians of the vast seas.

These beautiful creatures, once noble unicorns of the kingdom, had taken on a different guise, assuming their new roles as protectors and custodians of the Earth's precious waters. Alongside their aquatic brethren, other unicorns had chosen a different path, embedding their essence into the light codes of chosen humans, destined to carry the legacy of the unicorns within their very souls.

Driven by their unwavering love for their lost companions, King Orion and Queen Seraphina knew they must find a way to reach out to the transformed unicorns and infuse them with the awakening unicorn light. They believed that by doing so, they could awaken their memories and unite the oceanic realm and a new generation of humans with the magic of the Unicorn Kingdom and, eventually, bring Acacia back to life.

A magnificent council was convened in the heart of the Unicorn Kingdom. Beings of pure light and wisdom, including celestial beings and cosmic wizards, answered the call. They brought with them the knowledge of their respective realms, each possessing a unique piece of the puzzle.

.Five.
Quest for Princess Acacia

5

Years turned into decades, and decades turned into countless centuries. The memory of unicorns faded from the minds of humans and all beings, and the Earth's connection with the galaxy remained lost. But deep within the hearts of those who still believed, a glimmer of hope remained—the hope for the awakening of Princess Acacia.

Underneath the vast ocean, the transformed unicorns, now in their massive bodies, continued their vigilant watch. They swam as a group, their immense presence as a beacon of the unicorn kingdom's wisdom. They tirelessly searched the depths, their light bodies radiating a gentle glow, hoping to find any trace of the crystal form that Princess Acacia had been trapped in.

The Mermaid Kingdom

Tales of the enchanted stone that had caused great waves when it first descended into the ocean's depths captivated the merfolk, the residents of the mermaid kingdom, stirring their curiosity. Word of its otherworldly allure and hidden magic echoed through the pearl-laden halls of their underwater domain.

The mermaid kingdom existed in a unique dimension, veiled from the prying eyes of humans who roamed the surface world. It was a realm where time danced to its own rhythm, where the play of light and shadow wove intricate patterns upon the ever-shifting seafloor. The merfolk, guided by their inherent wisdom, knew that interactions with humans needed to be cautious and deliberate.

Sometimes, driven by their profound love for the ocean and the desire to share its wonders, mermaids and mermen would embark on secret missions. Slipping through the veil that separated their realms, they would swim among humans with a deep affinity for the sea. With their minds linked through telepathic connections, they would transmit ancient oceanic knowledge and tender messages of harmony, inspiring a deep reverence for the marine world.

The merfolk possessed a remarkable capacity to disguise their true identities and preserve their existence from human detection. The mermaids' dazzling pearl-white scales would refract and mingle with the surrounding currents as the brilliant light from above pierced the water's surface, producing an illusionary dance of liquid sunshine. This clever adaption made them practically undetectable, their existence hidden within the dazzling expanse.

Enthralled by the stone's potent energy and the ethereal glow that radiated the mermaids and mermen embarked on a daring expedition to retrieve it from the human realm. As their eyes beheld the stone, a collective gasp escaped their lips, and they found themselves entranced by its captivating allure. Like a celestial kaleidoscope, it shimmered and transformed, revealing an enchanting display of iridescent hues that danced and played within the ever-shifting currents of the underwater realm.

Despite its rough and weathered exterior, incapable of concealing the true magnificence that resided within, the stone beckoned the mermaids and mermen with an irresistible allure. As their eager hands grasped the rock, they felt a surge of energy coursing through their very beings, awakening a profound connection to the cosmos beyond what they knew of the elemental forces of the ocean. Though marred by time and the trials of its journey, its surface held a hidden splendor that defied all expectations. Each touch revealed a glimpse of its inner radiance as if the stone carried the universe's secrets within its rugged facade.

The stone was stored secretly in the mermaid kingdom for countless centuries, defying all attempts to unlock its mysteries by the past Queens. It remained an enigma, guarded with the utmost care, for its unfathomable power was a source of wonder and concern.

The current Queen, Meridia stood as a beacon of wisdom and grace within the mermaid kingdom. Adorned in a flowing gown that changed colors according to the ocean environment, her attire mirrored the vibrant hues of the coral reefs and the shimmering blues of the open sea. As she moved, her cascading sapphire hair caught the light, reflecting the ocean's depths as it seemed to hold the secrets of the underwater realm within its strands. Pearls of iridescent splendor graced her royal crown, each one a representation of her illustrious ancestry and deep connection to the ocean's vastness.

The centerpiece of Meridia's regal crown was a rare and exquisite gem, a cherished family heirloom passed down through generations. Known only to a select few, this gem held a hidden power. This secret resonated with the very essence of the mermaid kingdom. Its transcendental glow shimmered with an otherworldly brilliance, captivating all who beheld it.

The gem's true nature remained veiled, known solely to Meridia and those entrusted with the ancient wisdom of their lineage. It was said this gem could amplify Meridia's connection to the dimensions, enhancing her mystical gifts and unlocking deeper insights into the mysteries of the ocean and the cosmos. Its presence on her crown symbolized her noble lineage and the profound responsibility she bore as the guardian of her people and the keeper of their ancient knowledge.

Meridia possessed a special gift bestowed upon her by the ocean itself. With excellent knowledge of dimensions and a profound understanding of the cosmic intricacies, she could set up an impenetrable energy shield around her kingdom. This protective barrier ensured her people's safety and security, warding off intruders who sought to disturb the tranquility of their underwater paradise. Guided by her innate wisdom, Meridia used her gift to weave the ocean's energies and create a shield that harmonized with the natural rhythms of the sea.

Everyone sought Meridia's guidance and wisdom, and her regal presence brought a sense of calm and harmony to the mermaid kingdom. Her mesmerizing voice carried the echoes of ancient melodies woven with enchantments that commanded respect and reverence from her subjects. Under her benevolent rule, her subjects flourished, basking in the protective embrace of their queen and the boundless beauty of their ocean home.

☆

Queen Meridia had long yearned to uncover the stone's secret, unlocking its ancient knowledge and harnessing its dormant magic. She was acutely aware of the risks that came with it, even as her heart whispered promises of hope and evolution. The stone held immense power, bringing balance and harmony to their world. Still, its mishandling could unleash chaos upon the ocean. Her primary duty as Queen was to her people and the delicate ecosystems of the underwater realm.

Understanding the stone's paramount

importance, Meridia took swift action to protect it. She discreetly concealed the rock within the mermaids' secret chamber, a hidden sanctuary accessible only to the chosen merfolk. To further safeguard it, she encased the stone within an Energy Light Shield, bolstered by potent spells designed to ward off prying eyes. These enchantments had long shielded the mermaids from human detection, shrouding their existence in mystique.

With great care, Meridia entrusted the mission of unlocking the stone's secrets to Orville, her most trusted advisor, a wise seahorse. She believed in his wisdom and ability to decipher the enigmatic myths concealed within its ancient engravings.

"Orville, this is a critical mission," Queen Meridia said solemnly, her eyes reflecting the task's weight. "For countless centuries, we have tried to unlock this stone's secrets, but its mysteries have remained elusive. Legend speaks of a giant wave that swept over the ocean when the stone fell into its depths, and since then, the life forces in the world have diminished."

Meridia continued, "Our once vibrant world has grown fragile over time, and we had no choice but to protect ourselves within our realm, avoiding any interaction with other mystical beings."

As Queen Meridia looked at Orville with purpose, he nodded in understanding. He responded, "I understand, Your Majesty," speaking with intent. "This stone may hold the key to restoring the vitality to our realm and the ocean."

Orville was an unusual and enormous hermaphrodite seahorse with a remarkable ability to change his appearance. He was not only a wise and knowledgeable being but also served as the ambassador of the mermaid kingdom. With his extraordinary ability to adapt and transform his appearance, he became a trusted advisor, a beacon of wisdom, and a comforting presence for all who sought his guidance.

In his esteemed position as the oceanic sage, Orville would dispense profound insights and share his boundless understanding of the ocean's enigmatic wonders. Mermaids would converge around him, their tails undulating in eager anticipation as he unfolded the depths of his wisdom with eloquence and serenity. His voice, akin to the soothing murmur of the tides, resonated with the accumulated knowledge of ages, unveiling the secrets and intricacies of the underwater realm.

But Orville's influence extended beyond being a source of wisdom. He had a compassionate side that endeared him to the merfolk. Many mermaids sought his company to find solace and companionship. With a heart as vast as the ocean, Orville would change into a loving grandmother-like figure, offering a listening ear and a comforting presence. His mere presence brought peace and belonging, and mermaids often found solace in his embrace.

Orville's wisdom, adaptability, and compassion made him a beloved figure among the merfolk. His presence served as a unifying force, bridging gaps between different kingdom factions and fostering harmony. Mermaids would gather around him, their eyes shimmering with admiration and gratitude, as they sought his guidance, shared their concerns, and celebrated their triumphs.

Guided by the wisdom of Orville, the merfolk devoted their efforts to unraveling the secrets held within the stone. They delved into ancient scrolls and consulted the depths of their collective knowledge, searching for clues that would unlock its mysteries.

Lily's Dream

At the same time, on the surface of the Earth, humans carried on with their lives, oblivious of the existence of unicorns and the enormous magic they formerly brought. Unicorn stories became legends and bedtime stories as the generations went on. Yet, the last group of unicorn guardians, embedded in the DNA of chosen humans, patiently waited for the day Acacia would be found.

Among these humans was a young girl named Lily, who had been experiencing vivid dreams since she was a child. She would find herself immersed in enchantment and wonder in these dreams, where golden unicorns radiated an illuminating, shimmering light. These dreams often occurred during the full moon, as though the celestial body was beckoning her.

From a tender age, Lily felt an inexplicable connection to these dreams. They felt like a calling, a glimpse into a hidden world beyond everyday life's boundaries. During her nocturnal journeys, she would frolic alongside majestic unicorns, their golden manes dancing in the ethereal glow. The colors were more vibrant, the light more luminous, and a sense of purpose resonated deep within her heart.

One particular dream stood out among the rest. Lily found herself standing on the sandy shores of a magnificent ocean under the silver rays of the full moon. The waves whispered ancient secrets, carrying a melody only her soul could comprehend. A gentle voice echoed in her mind, resonating with otherworldly wisdom.

"Lily, you possess a special purpose," it whispered. "Seek the stone that lies beneath the sea. It holds the key to awakening Princess Acacia and restoring the forgotten magic of the unicorns."

When Lily awakened from this profound dream, her determination surged like an unstoppable tide.

She was consumed by an insatiable curiosity, yearning to unravel the mysteries hidden within her visions. It seemed the voice in the dream had ignited a spark within her that compelled her to seek answers and uncover the truth. With unyielding resolve, Lily delved into ancient unicorn legends, diligently scouring libraries and old documents for any information that could shed light on her dreams.

Lily's connection to the ethereal realm expanded beyond her dreams as she grew older. She discovered she possessed a remarkable gift—a voice that could only be described as angelic. From the moment she opened her mouth to sing, a captivating melody would flow forth, carrying divine resonance that touched the hearts of all who heard it.

This remarkable gift drew animals to her as she sang. Deer would approach, their eyes filled with curiosity and wonder. Butterflies would flutter gracefully, dancing in harmony with the melody. Even the gentlest creatures, like rabbits and squirrels, would venture near, their movements synchronized with the rhythm of her song.

A magical transformation unfolded as Lily's melodious notes filled the air. The forest came alive with music as if every creature and element joined in a symphony orchestrated by the unseen hands of nature. Inspired by her heavenly voice, the birds lent their melodic tunes, their songs intertwining seamlessly with hers. The air resonated with the harmonious blend of human and avian voices, creating an enchanting choir that echoed through the ancient trees.

The rhythmic beat of Lily's song would set the tempo for a grand orchestra of nature. The rustling of leaves became a gentle percussion, the babbling brook harmonized with its soothing melody, and the wind whispered a soft accompaniment. In this enchanted symphony, even the smallest creatures found their voice. From the chirping crickets to the croaking frogs, each added its unique sound, creating a tapestry of melodies that painted the forest with vibrant hues.

Together, they formed an orchestra of nature, a breathtaking collaboration between the human and natural world. The intertwining melodies and harmonies carried on the wind, spreading a sense of awe and wonder throughout the tranquil forest. It was a moment where boundaries blurred, and the line between singer and listener vanished, as all beings united in the universal language of music.

Lily's singing became a bridge, a cosmic concert connecting the land and sky. Her voice carried messages of love, hope, and unity, touching the souls of those who heard it. It seemed Lily tapped into a deep well of universal harmony, resonating with the very heartbeat of the Earth and the celestial realms beyond.

As Lily continued to explore the depths of her gift, she realized the responsibility it carried. She understood that her voice had the power to heal, uplift, and awaken the dormant magic within others. With each heartfelt note she sang, she brought a little more enchantment back into the world, reminding humanity of the long-forgotten wonders hidden in the realm of legends.

Little did Lily know that her extraordinary voice would play a pivotal role in the destined reunion with Princess Acacia and the restoration of Earth's magic.

The Riddle of Lightening

Back in the deep ocean, Orville, the seahorse, embarked on a tireless quest to unlock the secrets of the enchanted stone. He moved through the maze-like coral reefs with grace and agility, where schools of shimmering fish graced the beautiful underwater world with their brilliant hues. The bioluminescent creatures cast a magical glow, illuminating Orville's path as he sought the wisdom of the deep.

Guided by his intuition, Orville sought encounters with the venerable sages of the sea. He conversed with ancient sea turtles, their wise eyes reflecting the wisdom of countless tides. Their majestic shells, adorned with intricate patterns, seemed like portals to the realms of forgotten knowledge. Together, they delved into the hidden recesses of underwater caves, where the echoes of mysterious currents whispered ancient secrets of the ages.

As Orville journeyed through the ocean's vast expanse, he encountered an array of enigmatic creatures, each with profound insights. Among them were the wise octopuses, masters of disguise and masters of the art of adaptation. With their mesmerizing displays of camouflage, they revealed the secrets of blending seamlessly with their surroundings, becoming one with the vibrant coral reefs or vanishing into the shifting sands of the ocean floor. Through their teachings, Orville understood the delicate balance between visibility and concealment and the importance of adapting to ever-changing circumstances in the vast underwater realm.

Amidst this grand odyssey, Orville's travels unveiled the vast tapestry of wisdom woven into the ocean's depths. Each encounter enriched his understanding as he absorbed the diverse perspectives of the sea's wise inhabitants. With each revelation, he grew closer to unraveling the stone's enigmatic power, guided by the collective wisdom of the marine kingdom.

One fateful day, a bolt of lightning, unlike any other, struck the hallowed grounds of the mermaid sanctuary, where the cherished rock of Acacia was safeguarded. In an instant, the tranquil haven was ablaze with a mesmerizing display of radiant diamond lights, casting an enchanting glow upon the sacred space. The mermaid guards, awestruck by the spectacle, hastened to summon Orville, the keeper of ancient wisdom and guardian of the sanctuary.

"Orville, the stone was struck by lightning," one of the guards rushed to say.

"That's peculiar," Orville muttered in confusion as the guards swiftly informed him. "The regular lightning wouldn't pierce the water's surface and find its way to our shield realm. There must be something happening."

With a sense of urgency, Orville hurried to the scene, his heart racing with anticipation. As he approached the rock, his eyes widened in astonishment, for there, etched into the surface, was a riddle that had remained hidden from him until this moment. The revelation held the promise of untold mysteries and unforeseen paths yet to be explored. Its ancient script is etched into the very essence of the ocean. The words shimmered with an iridescent glow, captivating Orville's gaze. The inscription contained an enigmatic riddle, its cryptic words an invitation to unravel the stone's secrets and unlock the path to their ultimate destination.

"In the realm where stars meet the sea,
A quest for seekers sworn to be.
In a place where waves have gone,
Listen for the chant of early morn.
Where coral blossoms gleam and sway,
The path to secrets shall mark the way."

Coral Garden of Illusion

The riddle ignited a spark of recognition within Orville's wise mind. With a flash of remembrance, he recalled a place in the vast oceanic expanse—the Coral Garden of Illusion. It was a realm of enchantment, where the coral blossomed with a resplendent radiance, each blooming a mesmerizing kaleidoscope of colors.

Legends whispered of its magical properties, capable of unveiling hidden truths of the universe and amplifying the energies of those who dared to venture within. Orville believed this sacred place held the key to their next step on the mystical quest, where illusions danced with reality and secrets were waiting to be unveiled.

.Six.
Sanctuary of
the Doga

6

Chamber of Eternity

Deep within the vast ocean, concealed by an intricate network of underwater caves and mystical currents, lay the Doga sanctuary — a unique ethereal realm of breathtaking beauty and ancient secrets. The sanctuary's entrance was guarded by towering rock formations adorned with phosphorescent algae, their luminescent glow guiding the way for those fortunate enough to discover this hidden haven.

The Doga sanctuary was unlike any place on Earth. Its ethereal nature allowed it to transcend the boundaries of the deep ocean, connecting with the cosmic energies that permeated the universe. This mystical connection enabled the sanctuary to bask in the radiant light of the sun and the gentle embrace of the moon. With its golden brilliance, sunlight filtered through the water, casting enchanting patterns of dappled light that danced upon the sanctuary's coral garden.

As explorers ventured deeper into this underwater paradise, they were met with a kaleidoscope of vibrant colors. Coral reefs stretched as far as the eye could see, their intricate structures housing myriad marine life. Exotic fish, their scales shimmering in iridescent blues and fiery oranges, darted through the vibrant tapestry of coral. Graceful sea turtles lazily glided by, seemingly caught in a tranquil dance. Rays of sunlight filtered through the water, refracting and casting an iridescent glow upon the reef, creating an illusion of shifting shapes and shimmering mirages.

The Doga sanctuary possessed a magical aura, concealing its depths from prying eyes. Its vibrant colors took on a heightened brilliance as if nature had painted them with an ethereal brush. An enchanting illusion seemed to materialize, captivating the senses and discouraging any intrusions from outsiders. Delicate currents swirled around the towering rock formations, creating a mesmerizing dance of water and light obscuring this hidden realm's entrance.

But the Doga sanctuary truly came alive during the serene nights when the moon held dominion over the sky. With its silvery luminescence, the moonlight poured into the depths, illuminating the sanctuary with a mesmerizing glow. It bathed the Coral Garden, turning them into a spectacle of ethereal beauty, where colors shimmered, and aquatic life thrived in harmonious splendor.

The connection to these celestial luminaries within the sanctuary was not merely a reflection but a profound interaction. The coral blossoms responded to the moon's gentle touch, unfolding their petals in gratitude. The aquatic creatures swam in intricate patterns, a celestial ballet choreographed by the moonlight's embrace. It was as though the sanctuary was a bridge between the mortal realm and the celestial heavens, a sacred focal point where the magic of the ocean and the wisdom of the cosmos intertwined in an eternal dance.

In this enchanted realm, secrets of the ages lay hidden among the coral, waiting for those who sought its wisdom. The Doga sanctuary held the answers to questions not yet asked, and its radiant beauty was a testament to the timeless magic that dwelled beneath the ocean's surface.

In the heart of the sanctuary, there was a magnificent underwater city. Elaborate structures, crafted from luminescent opals and precious gemstones, glistened with an otherworldly radiance. A breathtaking luminescent waterfall cascaded from an unseen source above the city's central chamber. Its cascading waters shimmered with a gentle luminescence, casting a mesmerizing glow upon the Doga as they gracefully swam beneath its radiant curtain. This sacred waterfall was believed to hold the key to unlocking the most profound memories of their celestial origins, and each visit to the sanctuary's heart rejuvenated their connection to the Cosmos.

Deep within the underwater city's depths lay a hidden and sacred chamber that held the secrets of an ancient and highly developed civilization. This chamber, known as the "Chamber of Eternity," was said to be the nexus of cosmic energies. In this place, time and space intertwined in a dance of mystical power.

Legend spoke of a time when the unicorns discovered this chamber, long before their transformation into the majestic creatures that now graced the Earth's oceans. These ethereal creatures, with their bodies emanating a soft luminescence, were beings of pure light and enchantment. Having traversed the celestial planes, they yearned for a connection to the physical world and an intimate experience with the touch and sensation of the ocean's vibrant embrace.

Driven by an insatiable curiosity and an unquenchable desire to explore the unknown, the unicorns embarked on a momentous voyage to Earth. As they descended from the heavens, their radiant presence cast a gentle glow upon the waters below. They reveled in the anticipation of what lay ahead, their spirits filled with an indescribable eagerness to immerse themselves in the ocean's resplendent vibes. As they neared the earthly realm, an enchanting coral labyrinth appeared in the deep blue sea. Its intricate beauty beckoned to them as if it held the ocean's secrets within its very core.

As the unicorns drew closer to the earthly realm, their celestial gaze beheld the mesmerizing sight of an enchanting coral labyrinth nestled in the embrace of the deep blue ocean. Its beauty radiated with an irresistible allure. It seemed to guard the ancient secrets and mysteries of the vast oceans within its very core. They ventured into the labyrinth's heart, their bodies shimmering in harmony with the vibrant hues of the coral. They had stumbled upon a shimmering gateway concealed within the heart of a coral labyrinth. They were transported to an otherworldly realm of golden splendor and sacred chanting as they passed through the gateway.

The unicorns experienced a profound connection to the ocean's embrace in this golden realm. Their light bodies intertwined with the water, creating a mesmerizing display of shimmering radiance. They marveled at the playfulness of the waves, the kaleidoscope of colors that adorned the underwater tapestry, and the ethereal songs that resonated through the depths.

In that transcendent moment, the unicorns knew they had discovered something extraordinary. This encounter with the ocean's vibe and the secrets of the Chamber of Eternity would forever shape their destiny.

Full moon Ceremony

Within the Chamber of Eternity, the walls bore intricate carvings depicting celestial constellations and cosmic events, each symbol a hidden key to unlocking profound universal knowledge. At the heart of this sacred space rested the colossal "Chanting Meteorite," a golden disk intricately engraved with ancient sacred symbols. The vibration caused by the graceful swimming of Dogas filled the chamber, infusing the surroundings with celestial electric energy. The meteorite hummed with a presence that seemed to echo the universe, enveloping the chamber in sublime harmony. The Doga cherished their connection to the underwater city and the sacred Chamber of Eternity. They understood the immense responsibility entrusted to them and dedicated their existence to preserving the sanctity of this mystical realm. The secrets they guarded within these hidden depths were key to restoring the cosmic balance and ushering in a new era of enlightenment and wonder.

During the full moon, Doga performed moonlit bathing ceremonies within the Chamber of Eternity, their enormous bodies gracefully moving harmoniously with the mystical energies that permeated the sacred space. The true power of their connection to the cosmos unfolded during these awe-inspiring rituals. As the Doga encircled the Chanting Meteorite, a sacred golden meteorite intricately carved with holy chants, their melodic voices resonated perfectly with its ancient vibrations.

With each melodic chant that escaped their phonic lips, the chamber would come alive, bathed in a radiant glow that pulsed in sync with the universe's heartbeat. The sacred chants passed down through generations carried the echoes of celestial wisdom and cosmic secrets, infusing the Doga with a profound sense of purpose and transcendence.

As the Doga channeled their energies and intentions into the Chanting Meteorite, their bodies seemed to merge with the very fabric of the chamber. The golden hues of the meteorite intertwined with the luminescent glow of the Doga's bodies, creating an enchanting dance of light and energy. In this transcendent union, the physical and spiritual boundaries dissolved, and the Doga became conduits of celestial power, drawing upon the vast reservoirs of universal energy.

As their melodic chants reverberated throughout the Chamber of Eternity, the air seemed to shimmer with a flash of ethereal brilliance. The chamber's walls, adorned with intricate carvings and celestial symbols, pulsed with their own life as if mirroring the cosmic dance unfolding within. It was like the Doga and the Chanting Meteorite were conversing deeply with the universe, exchanging energies, wisdom, and visions.

As moonlight bathed the sanctuary during the full moon, celestial melodies resonated through the underwater city, reverberating off the walls and carrying the hopes and dreams of the Doga into the cosmic expanse. The harmonious symphony reached the ears of the sea creatures dwelling in the sanctuary, who, drawn by the magical allure, gathered around the Doga, their diverse voices blending in a harmonious chorus.

Amongst the sea creatures, luminescent jellyfish gracefully floated, their delicate tentacles pulsating with bioluminescent light, creating an enchanting spectacle. Intrigued by the Doga's ethereal presence, playful dolphins swam alongside them, creating intricate patterns in the water as they weaved through the currents. In this sanctuary, creatures of all kinds coexisted, bound by a shared reverence for the mystical power that emanated from the Doga.

These moonlit bathing ceremonies held a deep significance for the Doga, for in those sacred moments, they communed with the ancient spirits of their ancestors and forged a profound connection with the cosmic tapestry. They sought to restore balance, healing, and harmony to the Earth and beyond through their harmonious chants and the radiant energy they invoked.

The sanctuary remained hidden from human eyes, its existence known only to a select few who held a deep connection with the ocean's mysteries. It was a realm untouched by human influence, a testament to the resilience and determination of the Doga to protect their sacred space. Only during the full moon, when the tides and cosmic forces aligned, would the

Doga venture to the surface, bathed in moonlight, carrying the hopes and dreams of a world longing for the return of magic and harmony.

.Seven.
Mirror of Cosmic

7

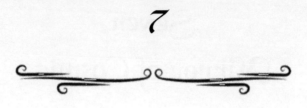

Lumina, the Cosmic Wizard

A sense of anticipation filled the air through King Orion and Queen Seraphina's diligent efforts and countless council meetings with the cosmic wise. The council chamber buzzed with otherworldly energy as illuminated beings from across the galaxies gathered to share their ancient wisdom and insights.

"Beloved King and Queen," Lumina's voice resounded with a profound sense of purpose as if every word carried the weight of cosmic significance.

Amidst the gathering, a figure draped in celestial robes stepped forward, her presence emanating a radiant aura that shimmered with iridescent blue, purple, and gold hues. Lumina, the wise cosmic wizard, stood before the council with eyes that sparkled like the starlit heavens, reflecting the accumulated knowledge of ages past. Her flowing robes, ethereal and weightless, seemed to mirror the vast expanse of the cosmos itself.

Adorned with intricate light patterns and symbols, Lumina's robes revealed the ancient secrets of constellations and nebulae. The celestial motifs danced and swirled across the fabric, captivating all who beheld them with their mesmerizing display of cosmic artistry. Each symbol whispered stories of distant galaxies and cosmic forces, a testament to Lumina's profound understanding of the universe's mysteries.

As Lumina moved, her robes came alive, illuminating with soft, shifting lights that mirrored distant stars' colors. The intricate patterns glowed with a gentle luminescence as they seemed to channel the very energy and wisdom of the cosmos. Those who gazed upon her attire couldn't help but feel a connection to the vast expanse of space and the ancient knowledge it held.

In Lumina's presence, the council members and all who witnessed her felt a deep reverence for the cosmic forces she embodied. Her celestial robes represented her immense wisdom and connection to the astral realms, infusing the chamber with wonder and awe. The council members, humbled by the cosmic artistry adorning Lumina's attire, knew they stood before a beacon of ancient knowledge, ready to guide them on their extraordinary journey.

"Throughout countless galaxies, I have ventured, witnessing the mesmerizing dance of celestial bodies and the ever-shifting currents of cosmic energies. Amidst my extraordinary odyssey, I have chanced upon a long-forgotten and potent ritual known as the 'Mirror of Cosmic' Within the depths of this ancient rite lies the potential to awaken the dormant light within our cherished planet Earth, Lady Gaia, and to unveil the sacred whereabouts of Princess Acacia."

The council members leaned in, their attention thoroughly captivated by Lumina's words.

She continued, "The 'Mirror of Cosmic' require all of us, the cosmic wise, to connect with our source roots and chant the birth sound of Source Light. By resonating the rhythm of planet Earth—a frequency that reverberates across dimensions—we can unlock the secrets of ancient events and glimpse possible future timelines that intertwine the universe and Earth."

As Lumina described the ritual, the council members felt a surge of anticipation and wonder. They understood that this resonance, this harmonious blending of cosmic energies and earthly frequencies, held the potential to awaken the sleeping magic within Lady Gaia. It was a call to ignite her remembrance and rekindle the powerful bond that had once existed between the celestial realm and the Earth.

The council members nodded in agreement, their eyes shining with renewed hope. Lumina's proposal held the promise of guiding them toward the answers they sought, leading them to the whereabouts of Acacia, the elusive presence hidden on planet Earth.

King Orion and Queen Seraphina exchanged a knowing glance, their hearts filled with gratitude for Lumina's wisdom. They realized that the "Mirror of Cosmic" held the key to restoring the sacred connection between Earth and the celestial realm. They gathered the cosmic wise with renewed determination to embark on this extraordinary journey of resonance and remembrance.

"Let us not delay any further, esteemed council members," King Orion's voice resonated with authority and eagerness as he addressed, "I invite each of you to join us in this crucial endeavor."

One by one, the council members nodded in acknowledgment, their faces reflecting enthusiasm and shared purpose. The gravity of the situation was evident to them all.

The universe seemed to respond as the council's intentions aligned with the cosmic energies. A rare celestial alignment graced the night sky as if the stars and planets echoed the divine council's goodwill. Lyra, Earth, and the Source formed a perfect triangle, their illuminated energies converging in a harmonious dance of cosmic unity.

The ethereal light cast a luminous glow upon the Unicorn Kingdom, infusing the air with a sense of wonder and possibility. It was a sacred time when the boundaries between realms blurred, and the wisdom of the celestial realm flowed freely into the realm of unicorns, embracing them in a divine embrace of cosmic interconnectedness.

The council members stood in awe, their gazes fixed upon the celestial alignment that adorned the night sky. Amazement radiated from their faces as they witnessed the power of their collective goodwill reflected in the cosmic dance above. The convergence of celestial energies seemed to affirm their purpose, filling their hearts with a profound sense of unity and purpose.

Lumina, her voice infused with cosmic resonance, spoke with unwavering conviction. "The time has come," she declared, her words carrying the weight of ancient wisdom. "Chant the birth sound of Source Light, merge the cosmic and earthly frequencies, and awaken the slumbering magic within Lady Gaia."

The council members took a deep breath, their souls attuned to the cosmic symphony surrounding them. One by one, they began to chant, their voices blending in perfect harmony. The melodies they sang were not of this earthly realm but a celestial language woven with stardust and cosmic vibrations. Each council member infused their unique galactic essence into the enchanting melody, igniting a symphony of heavenly sounds that resonated throughout the chamber.

As the heavenly melody swirled and danced, the space seemed alive. Beams of light intertwined with the harmonies, casting an ethereal glow upon the council members. The energy in the room grew palpable, as though the very fabric of time and space vibrated in response to the celestial resonance.

In this sacred moment, the council members were more than mere individuals. They were conduits of cosmic energy, channeling the wisdom of galaxies, ancient star systems, and celestial realms. Their unified song transcended language, bridging the gap between worlds and unlocking hidden gateways of knowledge and possibility.

In the kingdom's heart stood the Tree of Illuminations, a majestic tree that emanated a soft, ethereal light. Its illuminating branches reached towards the heavens, reflecting the celestial alignment above. Surrounding the tree, the council members formed a circle, their eyes shimmering with anticipation and determination. The air seemed to hum with cosmic vibrations as the universe breathed, waiting for the momentous resonance to begin.

Within the circle, the council members extended their hands towards the Tree of Illuminations, their fingertips gently touching its radiant bark. The tree responded to their touch, emitting a warm, pulsating light that intertwined with the cosmic energies in the night sky. The council's unity and the tree's mystical power created a powerful conduit, bridging the earthly and celestial realms.

Travel into Multiple Timelines

As the council immersed themselves in the cosmic mirrors' revelations, a breathtaking tapestry of timelines unfolded. They witnessed the ebb and flow of history on the Earth, the rise and fall of civilizations, and the intricate dance between chaos and harmony.

In one timeline, they witnessed the devastating destruction of the lands, where cataclysmic events reshaped the face of the planet. Wars ravaged nations, leaving scars upon the Earth's surface and the hearts of its inhabitants.

The world plunged deeper into darkness in another timeline, and the underworld's influence grew more vigorous. Unseen forces fueled by greed and power rose to prominence, manipulating the minds and hearts of humans. The Earth's natural balance was disrupted, and the delicate harmony between humans and nature was shattered.

Amidst the chaos and despair, a group of magical beings, including fairies, nymphs, and other ethereal creatures, retreated to the safety of hidden caves. These mystical sanctuaries provided refuge from the ravages of the outside world, shielding them from the hostility that permeated the Earth.

Despite the darkness, a ray of hope appeared. The mirrors revealed a future timeline in which a new Earth glistened with vibrant splendor. Unicorns, formerly assumed to be mythical creatures, have emerged in all their gleaming splendor. Magical beings of all types returned, their essence merging with the Earth's restored energy.

In this timeline, the council glimpsed the reconnection of a long-lost light portal, a gateway bridging the celestial realm and the Earth. Cosmic energies infused the planet through this portal, nourishing and revitalizing the lands. Lady Gaia, the spirit of the Earth, awakened from her slumber, resonating with the cosmic harmony that flowed through her.

As the cosmic mirrors shifted, the council beheld another remarkable sight. They witnessed the formation of an Earth Light Grid, a network of interconnected energy nodes established by awakened souls across the globe. These individuals, spread far and wide, were united in their dedication to anchoring light, love, and harmony upon the Earth. Through their collective efforts, a robust grid of positive vibrations enveloped the planet, radiating healing and transformation.

The council marveled at the diverse tapestry of timelines, each painting a unique picture of Earth's journey. They understood that Acacia's presence was intricately intertwined with the Earth's evolution and the cosmic forces at play. Acacia, the bearer of celestial lineage, held a key role in guiding the planet toward its destined path of light and renewal.

The council watched with bated breath as the cosmic mirrors revealed profound insights and glimpses into Acacia's journey. Excitement coursed through the council chamber, for they believed they were on the cusp of discovering Acacia's actual location. However, as the cosmic mirrors converged to unveil the final revelation, a mysterious light shade descended upon the chamber. It shrouded the images, obscuring the clarity they had longed for.

Confusion rippled through the council members as they exchanged puzzled glances. The cosmic resonance wavered, and the visions began to fade. The enigmatic shade seemed to hold secrets of its own, defying the council's attempts to decipher its meaning. A cosmic veil had been drawn, concealing Acacia's precise whereabouts.

Whispers filled the chamber, voices filled with a mix of frustration and determination. The council realized there was more to this quest than they had initially anticipated. The path to finding Acacia was veiled in mystery, demanding further exploration and understanding.

Undaunted, King Orion and Queen Seraphina requested a moment of contemplation, inviting the council to explore the depths of their cosmic wisdom. They sensed a hidden message behind the enigmatic shade of light, a puzzle that needed to be solved. They attempted to uncover this interruption's significance and purpose in their mission.

"Perhaps," a voice gracefully interjected.

As the council members quieted their voices, seeking inner guidance, a familiar voice emerged from the silence.

It was Andreanna, the venerable mentor of Acacia and a majestic unicorn being whose very presence radiated wisdom and grace. Her ethereal form stood tall and regal, her luminous violet hair cascading down her back in waves, each strand shimmering with a celestial luminescence rivaling the enchanting radiance of moonlight.

Andreanna's eyes, deep pools of ancient knowledge, held a gentle sparkle that hinted at the secrets she had within. The room fell into a hushed awe as her melodious voice filled the air, carrying the wisdom of ages and the guidance of the unicorn realms.

Throughout the ever-renewing journeys of Lady Gaia, Andreanna had stood as the unwavering beacon, guiding Acacia on her cosmic odyssey from its very inception. With gentle grace, Andreanna navigated Acacia through the labyrinthine paths of enlightenment, revealing the hidden truths within the mystical realms of unicorns and the revered Tree of Illumination. Under Andreanna's wise tutelage, Acacia's mind expanded, and her heart embraced the profound wisdom that flowed through the interconnected tapestry of existence.

"Acacia's path has intertwined with a mystical creature dwelling on planet Earth," she began, her words laced with a touch of ancient wisdom. "These creatures, guardians of their realms, have formed an ancient agreement to remain hidden from human eyes and undisturbed by each other's presence. Mermaids, dragons, griffins, phoenixes, and centaurs are among them, each with special magic and purpose."

The council members leaned forward, captivated by the mentor's words. The idea that Acacia might be kept by one of these mystical creatures opened up a realm of possibilities. It hinted at a deep connection between the cosmic realm and the Earth, where Acacia's presence was protected and concealed.

"We must delve deeper into the lore of these mystical beings," Andreanna continued, "for they hold the key to unraveling the enigma surrounding Acacia's whereabouts. Their ancient wisdom and hidden realms might provide the answers we seek."

The council members listened intently, their minds captivated by Andreanna's words. The realization dawned upon them that the elusive shade of light and the veiled presence of Acacia might be connected to this agreement. It became clear that the mystical creatures of Earth had created a dimensional shield, deliberately concealing themselves and Acacia from the view of the cosmic mirrors and the council's celestial gaze.

"Acacia possessed a gleaming diamond horn, a pure radiance conduit through which she could perceive the true essence of all beings," Queen Seraphina stepped forward, her regal presence commanding the council's attention. With a voice filled with both sadness and admiration, she spoke of Acacia's extraordinary gift that set her apart from other beings.

"Unlike humans, who are constrained by the complexities of their physical bodies, emotions, and intellectual challenges, Acacia's diamond ray can transcend these constraints. It enabled her to see through the layers that hid people's true natures, revealing their fundamental goodness. Her unclouded sense and staunch belief in the purity of all beings had led her to miss the presence of malice, leaving her vulnerable to human-set traps."

Queen Seraphina's words hung in the air, evoking wonder and empathy among the council members. They understood the magnitude of Acacia's gift and its profound challenges. It was both a blessing and a curse, for while Acacia could see the untarnished essence of every being, she was susceptible to the illusions and deceit woven by those who sought to exploit her boundless trust.

"This is exactly why those mystical creatures,

who deeply understood the complexities of living on Earth, had made an ancient agreement to protect themselves from human intrusion." Andreanna chimed in.

"Through their ancient wisdom and connection to cosmic energies, they devised a means to separate themselves from humans by existing in different dimensions. These dimensions acted as a barrier, shielding the mystical creatures and preserving the delicate balance between the celestial and earthly realms."

Andreanna continued, her voice full of comprehension. "Planet Earth has a one-of-a-kind tapestry of dimensions intricately woven with earthly elements and are highly dense. It is a domain in which the physical and astral coexist in a delicate balance. The dimensional shield ties together mysterious creatures to the physical Earth dimension, allowing them to remain concealed and secure.

However, a significant barrier has arisen for us pure light beings. The once-open light portal to Earth, which served as our connection and passage, has been abruptly closed, depriving us direct access to the earthly realm." Andreanna added, her gaze shifting across the assembled councils.

The council members exchanged concerned

glances, realizing the gravity of the situation. The closure of the light portal posed a formidable obstacle in their mission to bring healing and restoration to Earth. Their ability to aid and protect the Earth and its inhabitants seemed uncertain without a way to traverse the condensed dimensions and breach the now impenetrable dimensional shield.

Lumina, nevertheless, stepped out amid the uncertainty, radiating an aura of strength and drive. "Though the closure of the light portal presents a daunting challenge, it also invites us to seek new paths and unlock dormant abilities within ourselves," she said soothingly.

"We must explore other methods of entering the Earth realm and traversing the complex weave of dimensions that awaits us. We will explore hidden passageways and rediscover lost gatekeepers who may hold the key to breaching the dimensional shield with our collective wisdom and steadfast determination."

Her words ignited a renewed sense of purpose within the council members. They understood that the journey ahead would demand courage, resourcefulness, and an openness to the unknown. United by their shared vision, they vowed to forge ahead, seeking ancient wisdom and guidance from the celestial realms to find a way to penetrate the earthly realm despite the closure of the light portal.

King Orion walked forward, his royal presence commanding attention, his words echoing with a tone of unity and purpose.

"In our quest to find Acacia and restore balance to the Earth, we must tread upon this sacred realm with reverence," he declared.

"Let us honor the ancient agreements forged between our celestial kin and the mystical creatures who call this realm their home. Through cooperation and harmony, we shall navigate the intricate tapestry of cosmic and earthly magic that surrounds Acacia's presence."

With renewed determination, King Orion and Queen Seraphina invited the council members to share their knowledge and experience with these mystical creatures. They encouraged the exploration of ancient texts, legends, and encounters, seeking any hints or clues that could lead them to the elusive Acacia.

Kairos, the Master of Time

While the council members exchanged insights and shared their encounters with mystical creatures on

Earth, a figure clad in flowing robes emerged from the shadows. It was the Master of time, Kairos, a being whose age spanned millennia, yet his appearance remained eternally youthful.

As Kairos stepped forward, time seemed to ripple in his wake, creating an otherworldly aura of shimmering light that danced around him. The air crackled with subtle energy, carrying whispers of ancient prophecies and untold secrets. Dazzling sparks of luminosity encircled his form, casting a soft glow that pulsed with the rhythm of time's ceaseless march.

His presence commanded attention, for he was the guardian of the cosmic clockwork, the keeper of chronicles written in the language of the stars. Around him, the ebb and flow of time seemed to bend and weave, creating a surreal tableau that held the council members spellbound. His robes billowed gently as if moved by an unseen breeze, and intricate patterns of celestial constellations adorned the fabric, telling tales of cosmic alignments and divine dance.

As he addressed King Orion with a measured tone, his piercing glance contained the knowledge of eons. "King Orion," Kairos began, his voice resonating with a timeless authority, "Have you got in touch with the unicorns left on Earth?"

"Yes, we did," King Orion nodded, his eyes shining with gratitude and resolve. "We keep in touch with the unicorns who carry our essence by using the moonlight as a bridge."

"In exchange for the life on Earth to save Acacia, they had given up their precious light bodies and celestial existence," Kairos explained with a nod. "They acted incredibly bravely because they knew that time and space would confine them once they stepped into the complicated web of physical reality."

The council members' thoughts were filled with astonishment as they considered the intricate connections network that spanned time and dimensions. They marveled at the dedication of their unicorn brethren, who had taken on physical forms as Doga to navigate the earthly realm and those who had vanished into starlight codes.

"Indeed," King Orion affirmed. "They are glorious warriors, embodying the unicorns' essence of unconditional love," he exclaimed with profound admiration. "In a sacred realm where the constraints of time and space hold no sway, our unicorn Doga have discovered refuge and tranquility," he paused to let the significance of their role sink in before continuing. "Within this vortex, the past, present, and future borders blend into a harmonious totality. It allows us to constantly contact them, keeping their consciousness awake in physical form."

The Master of Time acknowledged, his eyes reflecting a new found understanding. "That's marvelous! The intertwining of all things is shown by the merging of past, present, and future within the vortex," he remarked. "It could serve as a conduit for the cosmic forces. Through this nexus, our connection with the Doga remains unbroken, anchoring the essence of the unicorn kingdom within the earthly realm."

Kairos' voice resonated with a timbre that seemed to echo through the very fabric of existence. As he spoke, a kaleidoscope of dazzling lights swirled around him, their vibrant hues pulsating with the rhythm of time. The luminescent display of colors depicts the interweaving threads of past, present, and future, symbolizing the intricate tapestry of cosmic interconnectedness.

With an outstretched hand, Kairos gestured towards the swirling vortex before them, its ethereal energy crackling with ancient wisdom. "Within this convergence lies the sacred nexus that bridges the realms of the unicorn kingdom and the earthly realm," he explained. "It is here that the Doga, guardians of timeless wisdom, serve as pillars of light, anchoring the essence of our celestial home within the depths of the earthly domain."

As the council members absorbed the wisdom of the Master of Time, their minds filled with possibilities and the realization that time itself could be manipulated for their quest. The Master of time continued, his voice resonating with the essence of eternity.

"Now, with the meeting of the Doga and Princess Acacia, both existing on Earth in the same time and space, a unique opportunity presents itself," the Master of Time declared. "By traversing the currents of time within the vortex, we can transcend the limitations of linear time. We have the chance to journey back to a moment when Acacia's crystallization had not yet occurred when she roamed the earth as a radiant unicorn. In that sacred juncture, we can imbue her diamond unicorn horn with a light code containing a message of the vortex. This enigmatic omen will resonate with her throughout her future journeys." Kairos explained.

"Why didn't we shift the timeline when the magician captured Acacia if we could influence the course of events?" Ambrose inquired, his tone tinged with both perplexity and curiosity.

Being from the Arcturus, a planet renowned

across the cosmos for its people's unmatched strength and might, Ambrose had a natural aptitude for pursuing knowledge and solving the universe's riddles.

Kairos, the revered Master of Time, met Ambrose's gaze with an air of profound wisdom. His gentle voice carried a depth of understanding as he unraveled the intricate nature of temporal manipulation.

"We have the power to influence events that occur within the timelines we have witnessed," he began, resonating with an aura of ancient knowledge. "Regrettably, we have not encountered any timeline where Acacia returned to Lyra. Some occurrences are intertwined with the fabric of destiny for reasons beyond our comprehension. Our abilities to alter events are limited to the open timelines, where the threads of possibility are still unfurled."

The council members absorbed his words, their thoughts swirling with newfound understanding. The intricacies of time and its enigmatic tapestry unveiled before them, urging them to contemplate the delicate balance between free will and preordained fate. They realized that their journey held the potential to reshape the course of history. Still, certain moments were bound by a higher design, evading their grasp.

At that moment, a sense of acceptance settled upon the council. They embraced the limitations of their temporal influence, recognizing that not all chapters of the cosmic narrative were meant to be rewritten. Their focus shifted towards the open timelines, where their collective efforts could mold the future with malleable hands. With resolute determination, they prepared to embark on their quest, knowing they could forge a path toward a brighter tomorrow within the realm of infinite possibilities.

Lumina, the wise cosmic wizard, moved forward again, her eyes gleaming with ancient knowledge. "In our quest to bring forth the diamond ray and elevate Lady Gaia to new heights, we must embrace the profound responsibility that comes with manipulating time," she emphasized. "We have explored the enormous webs of timelines, witnessing both the darkest times and the most glorious epochs on Earth. Through our collective wisdom and conscious choice, we must navigate the delicate balance of cause and effect."

With a deep breath, Lumina continued, "By entering the vortex, we enter the realm of infinite possibilities. It is a realm where time dances in harmonious convergence, allowing us to shape and mold its currents. We must tread this path with utmost reverence and awareness, for the repercussions of our actions will ripple through the fabric of existence. In this sacred act, we will reclaim the diamond ray and facilitate Lady Gaia's ascension."

Infused with determination and purpose, King Orion addressed the council once more. "Let us heed Lumina and Kairos' words and embrace the weight of our task. Together, as cosmic beings bound by love and responsibility, we shall embark on this extraordinary journey through the vortex. Guided by the divine forces, we shall inscribe Acacia's diamond unicorn horn, infusing it with the guidance to awaken her cosmic power. May our intentions be pure, and our actions be in harmony with the highest good of all."

The council members united in their commitment and stood tall and resolute. They understood the gravity of their mission and the potential it held to shape the destiny of both Acacia and the Earth itself. With hearts filled with hope and determination, they prepared to embark on their transcendent voyage through the vortex, where time would become their ally, and the riddle of light code would ignite a transformative journey for all involved.

Vortex without Time and Space

With a solemn expression, Kairos interjected, his voice resonating with caution and wisdom. "Dear council members, as we step into the vortex where time and space cease to exist, we must prepare ourselves for the extraordinary. The memories of our linear timelines across countless galaxies may resurface within its depths, revealing connections that span lifetimes," Kairos stated.

"We may encounter allies and adversaries, lovers

and kin from past eras. But we must not be trapped by the illusions of intertwined pasts, presents, and futures. If you find yourself disoriented amidst the swirling currents of time, listen closely for the primordial sound, the resonance of our shared origin. We shall find each other through its vibrations and navigate the enigmatic labyrinth as one."

His words hung in the air, a reminder of the potential perils and allurements that awaited them within the vortex. The council members exchanged glances, their eyes reflecting a mix of anticipation and trepidation. They understood that their journey would demand unwavering focus and inner strength. With a shared resolve, they vowed to stay vigilant, supporting one another as they delved into the abyss of timeless existence.

As the council members gathered around the Tree of Illumination, their hands trembled with a mixture of anticipation and trepidation. With a surge of collective energy, they focused their intentions on reactivating the Mirror of Cosmic, its surface shimmering with otherworldly light. The mirror, a portal to the cosmic realms, held the key to entering the vortex and unraveling the intricacies of time and space.

One by one, the council members advanced, their

forms gradually dissolving into ethereal essence. The Doga, majestic beings of immense power and grace, acted as conduits, bridging the connection between the vortex and the Tree of Illuminations. The council members entered the vortex through their unified presence, leaving behind the familiar confines of time and space.

Inside the vortex, reality transformed into a kaleidoscope of intertwined timelines. Past, present, and future melded together, creating a tapestry of cosmic events. Each council member had to find their inner center amidst the swirling chaos, focusing their mind and heart on the unity of their intentions.

However, as the council members delved deeper into the intricate dance of multiple timelines, the boundaries between their past and future became blurred. Memories and visions intertwined, threatening to unravel their grasp on reality. Some began to lose themselves in the labyrinth of their own existence, their sanity teetering on the edge of oblivion.

Amidst the growing confusion, Celestia, a luminescent being from Andromeda known for her extraordinary healing talents through the power of music and chanting, sensed the mounting distress within her fellow council members. With resolute determination, she stepped forward and closed her eyes, immersing herself in the symphony of cosmic energies resonating within the vortex. Her voice, pure and resonant, reverberated through the fabric of time itself as she chanted the melodious sound frequencies of her galaxy.

As Celestia's heavenly chant reverberated through the chamber, a wave of harmonic resonance spread outward, enveloping the council members. The angelic sound penetrated their beings, resonating with the core essence of their existence. Gradually, the cacophony of disjointed timelines receded, and a sense of clarity and serenity descended upon the council.

The council members awakened from their entangled visions one by one, their eyes flickering with newfound understanding. Celestia's melodic chant had served as an anchor, grounding them in the present moment and aligning their consciousness with the unified purpose that had brought them together.

With renewed focus and unity, the council members resumed their journey through the vortex, their determination fortified by Celestia's harmonious intervention. The labyrinth of timelines no longer threatened their sanity, for they now possessed the strength to navigate its complexities and extract the truths hidden within.

As they descended farther into the vortex, a gleaming timeline appeared, pulsing with the highest vibrations of love and harmony. It was the glorious timeline of Lady Gaia, where her essence radiated in its purest form. The council members concentrated their collective wishes towards this timeframe with unflinching determination, hoping to infuse it with the revitalizing force of the diamond ray.

Their consciousness traveled back to the moment when Acacia, adorned with her unicorn companions, called forth the diamond ray to heal and uplift Lady Gaia. It represented the unity of all beings, the harmonious coexistence between the celestial and earthly realms.

"It is now," Kairos firmly informed everyone, his voice resolute.

The council members began picturing an image in their minds — indicating a Doga sanctuary embedded within Acacia's horn. As their intentions grew stronger, a sudden lightning bolt struck the mermaid sanctuary where the rock of Acacia was kept. The impact resonated through the chamber, echoing the addition of this momentous event in the ancient scrolls of the Chamber of Eternity. It signified a timeline shift, merging destinies and fulfilling their purpose.

"We have completed our role here," Lumina stated confidently. "Let's keep our intentions high and ensure the hoped-for timelines are met. The universe will weave its magic, and the threads of destiny will continue intertwining."

With their mission accomplished, the council members surrendered to the vortex's flow, allowing it to carry them back to their realm of existence. They knew that the rest was now in the hands of the cosmic play, where the intricate interplay of energies and timelines would continue to unfold, guided by the forces of the universe.

King Orion and Queen Seraphina felt profound gratitude for the council members' efforts.

"Having you all gathered here is a great honor," King Orion expressed with sincerity. "Together, we shall restore the Source Light to Earth and bring Princess Acacia back."

And so, with hearts filled with reverence and gratitude, the council members emerged from the vortex, forever transformed by their journey. They returned to the council hall, their presence radiating the wisdom and power from traversing the realms beyond time and space.

.Eight.
Unveiling the Mystic Abyss

8

"**I found** it, I found it!" Lily screamed. Her outburst took all her friends aback, for she had always been known for her grace and gentleness. They gathered around her, curious about the cause of her sudden excitement.

Lily's hands trembled as she delicately held a weathered newspaper clipping, its page filled with the echoes of a long-forgotten tale. She continued with a deep breath to steady herself, her voice resonating with a captivating blend of enthusiasm and unyielding resolution. The sparkle in her eyes betrayed a glimmer of boundless adventure as she embarked on the extraordinary narrative.

"I understand that what I'm about to share may sound unbelievable," she began, her voice brimming with excitement, "but this incredible document unveils an extraordinary account from the journals of Hank Kahawai, a young and promising marine biologist. In his breathtaking discoveries, he recounts an encounter with majestic unicorns near the mystical Mariana Trench, a place known for its enigmatic depths and untold wonders."

Her friends exchanged incredulous glances, their curiosity piqued by Lily's extraordinary discovery. G.T., known for his logical thinking, raised an eyebrow, his skepticism evident.

"The Mariana Trench?" he questioned, his voice laced with doubt. "That's the deepest part of the Earth's oceans. Unicorns in such an extreme and inhospitable environment? It seems impossible."

"I thought unicorns were supposed to live in the forest," Drew chimed in, his voice barely above a whisper.

The group fell silent for a moment, contemplating the paradox of the situation. The image of gentle, magical creatures swimming in the deep, dark abyss of the Mariana Trench challenged their preconceived notions.

Undeterred by their skepticism, Lily met their doubtful gazes with a determined expression. "I understand your doubts," she said, her voice filled with anticipation and conviction. "But think about it. Unicorns have always been associated with purity and grace. Perhaps their presence in the Mariana Trench represents a hidden realm, an untouched sanctuary deep within the Earth's vast and unexplored oceans."

Her words hung in the air, inviting her friends to consider the possibility of a wondrous connection between unicorns and the ocean's depths. A sense of awe and intrigue settled upon the group as they contemplated these mythical beings' enigmatic nature and the mysteries hidden beneath the waves.

Lily's enthusiasm grew as she continued, her voice carrying a sense of adventure. "Professor Kahawai's account reveals that he dedicated years to researching the Mariana Trench, studying its unique ecosystem and the mysteries hidden within its depths. He embarked on numerous expeditions, braving treacherous conditions and pushing the boundaries of exploration.

In one of his voyages, while his boat was out of order, leaving him stranded on the ocean overnight,

Professor Kahawai found himself in a situation of unexpected wonder," Lily recounted, her voice filled with anticipation.

"As he lay resting on the deck, gazing up at the mesmerizing glow of the moonlight, a radiant luminosity began to emanate from the depths below. The moon, full and unusually vibrant that night, cast its ethereal glow upon the ocean's surface, painting the waves with a surreal luminescence. Professor Kahawai's gaze shifted from the celestial beauty above to the mysterious depths beneath, drawn by an otherworldly illumination that beckoned him closer."

At that moment, the group of friends could almost hear the soft whispers of the moon, like it held secrets untold. The moon's presence infused the air with mystery and possibility. They felt a deep connection to the night sky as if they were part of a grand cosmic dance where the moon and the ocean harmonized perfectly.

Lily's words vividly depicted this ethereal moonlit scene, fueling their imagination and igniting their desire to witness such enchantment firsthand. They yearned to stand on the deck of a boat, bathed in the silver moonlight, and gaze upon the luminous beauty that awaited them beneath the waves.

"Amid the abyssal darkness, his boat was

surrounded by bioluminescent creatures; he beheld a spectacle that defied imagination," she continued, her words weaving a tale of awe.

"The bioluminescent creatures shimmered like stars, creating a celestial tapestry that stretched as far as the eye could see. They emitted a soft, pulsating glow, their radiant light casting an ethereal ambiance in the underwater realm.

Professor Kahawai couldn't help but be drawn to the enchanting allure of the bioluminescent shimmering lights. With exhilaration coursing through his veins, he knew he had to explore further. Without hesitation, he dived into the water, submerging himself in the captivating realm beneath the surface.

Clusters of luminous plankton floated in delicate wisps, trailing behind him as he ventured deeper into the trench. Each movement of his hands stirred up a mesmerizing display of glowing trails, like a painter's brushstroke across a canvas of darkness. The water seemed to come alive with a symphony of colors. It felt like the very essence of magic had been captured in every bioluminescent particle.

Professor Kahawai's heart quickened with anticipation as he followed the path illuminated by the ethereal lights. The bioluminescent creatures danced around him, their radiant glow guiding him toward a hidden destination. With each stroke and kick, he felt connected to the mystical energy that permeated the underwater world.

The ocean's depths were alive with an otherworldly radiance, a symphony of colors and light," Lily continued, her words painting a vivid picture. "And there, amidst this ethereal spectacle, he witnessed a phenomenon unlike anything he had ever seen.

Suddenly, a breathtaking sight emerged before his eyes. A giant, vibrant coral structure stood tall and proud, its colorful branches shimmering like thousands of diamond rays. Professor Kahawai was awestruck, his gaze fixed upon this majestic spectacle. He couldn't help but feel a surge of reverence for the beauty and grandeur that surrounded him.

A subtle shift in the underwater realm caught his attention as he marveled at the coral's glorious display. The coral started to change color, shifting from vibrant hues to an iridescent kaleidoscope of shades. Quicker than he could respond, it seemed the coral had opened a portal to the galaxy's far reaches.

A magnificent panorama spread before him through this mesmerizing doorway. Countless stars dotted the immense expanse of space like gleaming diamonds. Nebulas swirled with vivid colors, painting the cosmos with ethereal brushstrokes. It was a sight beyond human comprehension, a look into the infinite grandeur of the universe.

The next phenomenon unfolded before Professor Kahawai as he took in this stunning sight. The elusive unicorns, bathed in the cosmic glow of distant galaxies, gracefully emerged from the shadows. Their presence was captivating and surreal, their luminescent bodies blending seamlessly with the cosmic backdrop.

As the unicorns moved with unmatched elegance, their luminous horns pierced through the blackness, illuminating the cosmic waters with an otherworldly radiance. It was a sight that defied all expectations, a fusion of terrestrial and celestial realms converging in a symphony of enchantment."

Lily's friends were now fully engrossed in the story, and their imaginations ignited with the possibilities.

G.T., the ever-curious mind, pondered aloud, "If unicorns truly reside in the Mariana trench, it raises countless questions about their adaptation to such extreme conditions. How do they navigate the immense pressure and the frigid temperatures? What secrets does the trench hold, and what connection do the unicorns have to this enigmatic place?"

"The bioluminescent creatures surrounding the unicorns created a breathtaking spectacle, their gentle glows intermingling and casting a vibrant, iridescent aura. The water itself seemed to come alive, teeming with a symphony of colors that danced and shifted with every movement. It was a celestial display as if the ocean had been transformed into a grand stage for the unicorns to showcase their ethereal beauty." Lily went on.

"Enraptured by the scene, Professor Kahawai found himself transported into a realm where reality merged with fantasy. The darkness of the night was illuminated by the radiant glow of the unicorns, their presence exuding an air of mystique and enchantment. In that transformative moment, the boundaries of what was deemed possible faded away, leaving only the undeniable truth of the unicorns' existence. But it wasn't just their serene beauty that captivated him," Lily added, her voice growing softer as if sharing a well-kept secret.

"The unicorns created a breathtaking display of magic and harmony. As their horns intertwined, they formed a radiant light tunnel, reaching from the ocean's depths to the surface above. The silver moonlight danced upon the water, casting an enchanting glow that bathed the entire realm.

The melody of an outer-world song filled the ocean, its celestial notes resonating through the water in a harmonious symphony. It was a melody that one could never find on Earth, a composition that transcended the boundaries of human understanding. The enchanting tune seemed to vibrate with the essence of the cosmos, creating a weaving of heavenly sounds that moved everyone who heard it to their cores.

As the song emanated from the unicorns, its captivating resonance reached far and wide, entrancing the hearts of all creatures that dwelled within the ocean's depths. Corals, adorned in their vibrant hues, swayed in synchrony, their branches pulsating with the rhythm of the celestial melody. Dolphins leaped with joy, their acrobatic displays harmonizing with the enchanting notes that filled the water.

An array of marine life, ranging from the tiniest fish to the most exotic anglerfish, came together in a mesmerizing dance encircling the unicorns. Every creature seemed to sway to the rhythm of an invisible symphony; their movements synchronized with the ebb and flow of the ocean's melody.

It was as if nature's choreography had woven

them into a harmonious ballet, celebrating the intricate interconnectedness of all life forms. The waters sparkled and glistened as their collective motion created a stunning display. This aquatic spectacle mirrored the beauty and unity within the ocean's depths.

Professor Kahawai felt an indescribable ecstasy at that moment. It seemed he had become one with the ocean. He felt the timeless rhythms and melodies of the underwater realm coursing through his veins, his very being entwined with the cosmic song. It was as though he had tapped into the universal language of the cosmos, understanding the interconnectedness of all existence."

A mischievous smile played across Wild's face as Lily finished recounting the magical scene. He couldn't resist teasing Lily, even in front of such wonder. "Are you sure he's not high on his deck?" he quipped, laughter lacing his words.

Lily's eyes widened in mock indignation, and a playful glint sparkled in her gaze. "Oh, Wild, you always find a way to bring humor to the most extraordinary stories," she replied, her tone filled with amusement. "But trust me, this was no ordinary sight. It was a moment of pure magic and awe, witnessed by a true explorer of the depths."

"Perhaps he's in a lucid dream or theta wave status," added Sara, raised in a new-age community. Her voice carried a hint of mysticism and possibility. "You know, the realm where fantasy merges with reality, where extraordinary encounters are possible. The fabric of dreams holds endless possibilities, where the boundaries of what we perceive as real blur. Perhaps Professor Kahawai, in his profound connection to the ocean, tapped into this metaphysical realm and caught a glimpse of a hidden world beyond our comprehension."

"Lucid dream? Someone, please take me back to Earth," Drew exclaimed, his face filled with confusion. He was always the pragmatic one, grounded in the tangible world. The concept of a dream-like realm merging with reality seemed far-fetched to him.

The group erupted in laughter, their shared bond strengthened by their playful banter. And yet, deep down, they all knew that there was more to Professor Kahawai's encounter than mere imagination. There was a spark of truth in the fantastical, a glimmer of possibility that urged them to embark on their own journey of discovery.

"There is only one way to find out," Giselle said, her voice filled with determination and adventure.

Her vibrant personality and love for exploration

were well-known among their close-knit friends. Giselle had been a close friend to Lily since childhood. While Lily embodied grace and gentleness, Giselle exuded a vibrant energy that sparked curiosity and fueled their shared adventures. Her eyes shimmered with excitement as she spoke, her enthusiasm infectious.

"Let's go to the Mariana Islands," Giselle declared, her voice carrying an air of excitement. "It is said to be a place where the boundaries between worlds are thin, where the mystical and the mundane intertwine. We might find clues if there is any truth to Professor Kahawai's encounter."

Her words resonated with a sense of possibility and sparked the imaginations of her friends. Giselle was known for her boundless optimism and unwavering belief in the extraordinary. She thrived in the face of the unknown, always eager to uncover hidden secrets and push the boundaries of their understanding.

"I am in," Fergus whispered, awakening from his nap with a low, appealing voice.

.Nine.
Queen Meridia and the Riddle

9

The Coral Garden of Illusion

"*In the realm where stars meet the sea,*
A quest for seekers sworn to be.
In a place where waves have gone,
Listen for the chant of early morn.
Where coral blossoms gleam and sway,
The path to secrets shall mark the way."

The kingdom hall was filled with an exciting air as Queen Meridia's ethereal voice resounded throughout. Her regal presence commanded attention as she recited the riddle of the rock, her words carrying a sense of mystery and anticipation.

The riddle possibly held the secret to unraveling the enigmatic path leading to the fabled Coral Garden of Illusion, a realm veiled in allure and peril. As Orville's discoveries had shown, it was a path that would not only guide them to the garden' breathtaking beauty but also reveal the profound secret hidden within the rock.

The merfolk listened intently, their eyes shimmering with intrigue and reverence, as they contemplated the riddle's cryptic message and its implications for their quest. The Coral Garden of Illusion held an allure that had captivated the hearts of Merfolk for generations.

Deep within its depths, a hidden underwater city was rumored to exist—a sanctuary where the forces of the cosmos intertwined with the magic of the sea. This underwater city was said to harbor knowledge and artifacts of immense power. It was guarded by mystical beings and ancient guardians who had pledged their allegiance to the Coral Garden. Now, with the riddle as their guide, they were on the precipice of unveiling the true essence of the stone and the untold treasures it held.

"People have long spoken of the Coral Garden of Illusion as a realm guarded by the Dragons," Queen Meridia began, her voice laced with caution and curiosity. Her azure eyes sparkled with the allure of the unknown, tinged with a deep understanding of the risks involved.

The Dragon's Illusory Labyrinth

Legends whispered of the Dragons, ancient beings of immense power who held dominion over the Coral Garden. They were said to possess the ability to shape reality itself, weaving intricate illusions that ensnared the minds of those who dared to enter without their permission. Once trapped within the realm, the boundaries between reality and fantasy blurred, merging in perplexing limbo.

The Dragons were not merely guardians of illusions. They were also the masters of bridging the ethereal and physical realms, owning the knowledge and wisdom to move between them with grace and harmony. Their connection to the Coral Garden ran deep, their essence intertwined with the mystical energies permeating the underwater kingdom.

Within their majestic forms resided the secrets of ancient magic, passed down through generations, their power harnessed for the betterment of their realm. The Dragons' ability to shape illusions was not a mere trickery, but a testament to their profound understanding of the intricate balance between reality and perception.

☆

"It is said a magnificent city hidden within the heart of the Coral Garden," Queen Meridia continued, echoing with reverence. "It is known as the Eternal City, a sacred space that holds the secrets of cosmic events and ancient prophecies." As she spoke, the gathering leaned in, captivated by the tale unfolding before them.

"The Eternal City exists beyond the veil of illusions, where reality merges with dreams," Meridia explained, her voice carrying an air of mystique. "Within its walls, time becomes elusive, and the boundaries of past, present, and future blur into one. Those who seek its wisdom must navigate the illusions that guard its entrance, for only those with pure intentions and unwavering hearts can access its profound knowledge."

As her words settled in the air, a hushed reverence fell upon everyone. The notion of a realm where time held no sway and the secrets of the cosmos were laid bare filled them with awe and trepidation. They knew their journey to the Eternal City would be ordinary. It would require courage and the strength to confront the illusions that would test the depths of their resolve.

Queen Meridia's voice carried a solemn note as she continued, her words a cautionary tale echoing through the chamber. "To venture into the Coral Garden without the Dragons' blessing is to risk losing oneself in the seductive allure of illusions, forever entangled in a labyrinth of one's fantasies." Her gaze shifted to those present, emphasizing the gravity of the situation.

Nadia, the chief of guards, stepped forward, her expression resolute yet tinged with a glimmer of hope. "The Dragons used to be our trusted allies before we closed our borders," she offered, her voice echoing with unwavering loyalty. "Perhaps they would grant us passage if we approach them humbly and seek their permission."

"In that case, we would expose the rock, and we are not sure of the unknown risks it might entail," Queen Meridia pondered aloud, her voice laced with caution and wisdom. Her eyes revealed a deep concern, reflecting the gravity of the situation.

"Furthermore, we have lost contact with the Dragons since the Earth lost its vitality long ago. They were once treasured allies, but time and fate have obscured their kingdom in uncertainty."

The weight of the decision hung in the air, and the group was immersed in deep contemplation. A hushed murmur spread through the hall as the merfolk contemplated Nadia's proposition.

In the past, the Dragons had maintained a delicate alliance with the mermaid kingdom. They had safeguarded the borders of the mermaid kingdom and offered their wisdom in times of need. However, the notion of revealing the rock's existence and their quest carried its own risks and uncertainties.

Queen Meridia's attention wandered to the sparkling gemstone on her crown as the gathering pondered. This valuable family relic held secret power. She remembered those stories about a long-ago relationship between her ancestors and the Dragons. The gem, a prized representation of her ancestry, carried mysteries that had not yet been fully exposed.

"There is another path," a voice resonated from the depths of the hall suddenly, intertwining wisdom and ancient knowledge.

Queen Meridia's contemplative gaze met Zephyr's knowing eyes, recognizing the glimmer of insight radiating from the kingdom's oldest and most revered merman.

Renowned as a guardian of hidden knowledge and a keeper of ancient lore, Zephyr held an intrinsic understanding of the ebb and flow of the sea's rhythms and the whispered secrets it carried. He had dedicated countless years to unraveling the enigmatic mysteries of their underwater realm and possessed a profound connection to the ocean currents.

His words held a weight derived from a lifetime of experiences as he addressed the group, commanding the attention of all those present. "Legends speak of a hidden passage, accessible only to those with hearts purest in their intentions and the courage to confront their deepest fears." Zephyr declared, his voice resonating with unwavering certainty.

The assembled leaned in, their fascination growing with each word that escaped Zephyr's lips. His knowledge of the mystical realms was unparalleled, and they hung onto his every syllable. Zephyr continued, his voice taking on a solemn tone.

The Call of the Void Nexus

Zephyr caught everyone's attention as their eyes grew

eager. He continued, his voice resonating with a sense of ancient wisdom. "Deep within the Void of Whispering, a phenomenon of great cosmic power exists—an ethereal vortex known as the Void Nexus. It is said to possess extraordinary abilities, capable of unveiling the deepest fears within one's soul. The Void Nexus is where ocean currents disappear, a place untouched by the watchful gaze of the Dragons," Zephyr revealed, his eyes carrying a profound understanding.

"When one enters the depths of the Void Nexus, their deepest fears embody and whisper relentlessly into their ears. The further they journey into its depths, the louder these whispers become, threatening to consume their courage and unravel their resolve." Zephyr's words hung in the air, heavy with the weight of truth and the ominous aura of the unknown.

The group exchanged uneasy glances, realizing the treacherous nature of the Void Nexus. They understood that this ethereal vortex was a realm where the darkest corners of their minds would be laid bare, where their deepest fears would be conjured and amplified. It was a place that demanded unwavering bravery and unyielding determination.

Paused for a moment, Zephyr allowed his words to sink in. His gaze swept across the faces of the meeting members, each one reflecting a mixture of apprehension and determination.

With a voice filled with unwavering conviction, he continued, "However, there is hope for those rare souls who possess the strength to embrace their darkness without succumbing to its allure. Those who can stand firm in the face of their deepest fears will be granted a unique opportunity—to experience the purest connection with the divine cosmic power that the Void Nexus conceals."

The assembled exchanged intrigued glances, realizing the significance of Zephyr's words. To confront one's deepest fears and emerge unscathed was no small feat, but the rewards promised were immeasurable. They understood that only those with a well-trained mind and an unwavering spirit could pass through the treacherous Void Nexus and access the secret chamber within the Coral Garden of Illusion.

In that chamber, legends spoke of celestial energies converging, illuminating the path to enlightenment and unlocking the mysteries of the cosmos. It was a place where time stood still, and the merfolk could glimpse the vast tapestry of the universe, woven with threads of stardust and pulsating with the rhythm of cosmic energy. It was an opportunity to commune with the celestial forces and harness their limitless potential.

As all of them contemplated the magnitude of the task, a sense of unease settled upon the chamber. While their hearts brimmed with a desire to explore the secrets of the Coral Garden of Illusion, many among them knew that their resolve might falter in the face of their deepest fears. The majority of merfolk, aware of the haunting whispers that awaited them in the Void Nexus, couldn't bear to confront their darkest thoughts. Fear held them in its grip, compelling them to turn away from the path that led to enlightenment.

At that moment, a wave of uncertainty washed over everyone, casting a shadow upon their aspirations. They were reminded of the rarity of those who possessed the unwavering strength to confront their inner demons. Only a select few merfolk, fortified by their well-trained minds and fortified spirits, would dare to venture deeper into the Void Nexus, determined to conquer their fears and seize the cosmic wisdom that awaited them.

They understood that this quest was not for the faint of heart or those seeking an easy path. It was a path reserved for the courageous few who dared to face their fears head-on and emerge victorious.

Amidst the hesitations that permeated the hall, a

voice broke through the uncertainty. Orville, known for his insatiable curiosity and unyielding spirit, stepped forward with a resolute expression.

"Count me in," he declared, his voice steady and determined. "In a place where waves have gone, listen for the chant of early morn." He repeated the riddle, pondering its meaning for a moment before continuing, "I believe it might refer to the Void of Whispering."

Queen Meridia nodded, her eyes filled with respect and compassion for Orville's chosen course. Her faith in his determination was steadfast, knowing that his quest for knowledge and unbreakable spirit would guide him through the hardships that were ahead within the Void Nexus.

"Your insight is truly acute," Zephyr acknowledged with approval. "The Void of Whispering is a realm shrouded in mystery, where the waves no longer exist. In the stillness of the Void, the echoes of the past and the whispers of the future converge."

Then, to the surprise of all there, another voice came from the assembly. Nadia, the chief of guards, was known for her unshakable dedication and bravery.

"I, too, will volunteer to embark on this perilous

journey," she said, her voice firm and determined. "Together, we shall face the depths of the Void Nexus and emerge stronger, fortified with the wisdom and power that it bestows."

A ripple of courage rippled through the members in the hall as Nadia's words hung in the air. More merfolk stepped forward, their determination blazing clearly in their eyes, inspired by the bravery showed by Orville and Nadia. One by one, they expressed their desire to join the risky mission, ready to put their skills to the test against the depths of the Void Nexus.

Among the brave volunteers, Evelina stood out as the most remarkable. Zephyr's gaze met hers as she confidently stepped forward, a silent recognition passing between father and daughter. Within Evelina resided a rare and extraordinary gift that set her apart from the other merfolk—an ability known as clairaudience. Through her acute senses, she could perceive the gentle whispers of the ocean, attuned to the subtle messages carried by its currents.

"I am in," Evelina said with a firm voice, full of solid will and faith.

Her eyes sparkled with an inner fire, reflecting her steadfast commitment to the arduous journey ahead. As she spoke, her fellow merfolk marveled at the strength and clarity of her conviction.

Zephyr nodded, showing his daughter with pride and confidence in the subtle curve of his smile.

Since her earliest days, Evelina had embraced her clairaudient talents, training diligently under her father's guidance. Through her connection to the mystical currents, she could perceive the secrets and wisdom that resided within them. Her ability to attune her ears to the hidden melodies of the ocean granted her profound insights into the challenges ahead.

Evelina's clairaudient talent was a source of wonder and admiration among her people. The ocean spoke to her in a language only a select few could comprehend, its secrets and wisdom unveiling through the ethereal melodies that caressed her ears. She possessed a deep understanding of the ocean's hidden depths, guided by the currents' murmurs and the whispers of ancient creatures that dwelled within.

With her unique talent, Evelina had an unmatched advantage in navigating the forthcoming challenges. As they ventured into the depths of the Void Nexus, where fears materialized and threatened to overwhelm, Evelina's attuned ears would listen with unwavering focus. Through the disorienting echoes and haunting whispers, she would discern the truths that lay obscured, guiding her companions with her intuitive perception.

The merfolk gathered in the hall regarded Evelina with admiration and anticipation. They recognized her tremendous power and the ability to decipher the secrets hidden within the ocean's whispers. With Evelina's clairaudience leading the way, their chances of safely traversing the treacherous path through the Void Nexus and unlocking the mysteries of the Coral Garden of Illusion soared to new heights.

Triton, a formidable warrior with a heart as mighty as the ocean currents, stood next to Evelina. "Count me in for this crucial mission, too," Triton said with charisma and assurance.

His towering stature and well-developed physique earned him the admiration of his peers. They made him an obvious choice for leadership. Triton's steadfast dedication to the realm and his fellow merfolk made him an indispensable squad member.

Evelina smiled warmly at her loyal friend and fellow warrior, acknowledging the significance of his commitment to the mission.

As more merfolk stepped forward, their collective resolve grew stronger, forming a bond forged by shared purpose and unspoken camaraderie.

Each member brought their unique strengths and talents to the table, creating a diverse group ready to face the unknown. Their determination fueled the council chamber with renewed hope and unity.

Queen Meridia looked upon the brave souls who had volunteered, her heart swelling with pride and gratitude. She knew the path ahead was treacherous, fraught with peril and uncertainty. But with this courageous team, she believed in their ability to overcome the challenges that lay before them and unlock the secrets of the Coral Garden of Illusion.

With a solemn nod, Queen Meridia addressed the assembled, her voice carrying the weight of her regal authority. "We stand united in our quest, bound by a shared purpose and unyielding determination. Together, we shall venture into the depths of the Void Nexus, confronting our deepest fears and embracing the cosmic wisdom that awaits. Let us embark on this journey, knowing that our courage will be tested, but our spirits shall remain unbroken."

As her words echoed through the hall, a renewed sense of purpose filled the hearts of all those present. The gathered members, volunteers, and Queen Meridia knew their path would be difficult. Still, they also knew that within the darkness of the Void Nexus lay the potential for profound transformation and enlightenment. They were prepared to face their fears, for they understood that they could only truly step into the light by embracing their shadows.

The Magic Shield

On their departure to the Void of Whispering, Orville carefully placed the rock in his brood pouch with tail, feeling its enigmatic energy pulsating against his entire body. The weight of their momentous mission settled upon the brave group as they congregated near the shimmering shores of the kingdom. Resplendent in her regal attire, Queen Meridia stood before them, exuding a captivating blend of solemnity and unwavering hope.

With elegant majesty, Queen Meridia addressed the brave group, her voice filled with unyielding strength. "I have crafted an extraordinary shield woven from the very fabric of magic waves that flow through our realm," she declared, her words carrying a resolute tone. "This energy shield will envelop you, safeguarding your journey and ensuring no external force can harm you."

Her gaze swept across the assembled merfolk and Orville, their eyes shimmering with anticipation and gratitude. "Within this shield, the harmonious convergence of ancient incantations and the ebb and flow of mystical energies intertwine," Queen Meridia continued, her voice resonating with a hint of reverence. "It forms an ethereal barrier that repels darkness and shields you from the malevolent forces that may seek to impede your path."

As she spoke, a vibrant display of magic waves appeared before their eyes, cascading in mesmerizing patterns of iridescent colors. The waves pulsed and undulated, emanating a soothing aura of protection. The merfolk marveled at the sight, awestruck by the tangible manifestation of their queen's power.

"Each of you possesses wisdom and courage that surpasses the depths of the ocean," Queen Meridia proclaimed, her voice filled with unwavering confidence. "May this shield be a testament to the courage within each of you, guiding your path as you unravel the secrets held within the rock and the Eternal City. Your triumphant return will be a beacon of hope and inspiration to all who dwell in our kingdom."

The merfolk nodded in solemn agreement, their hearts swelling with a newfound sense of purpose. They understood the magnitude of the shield's creation and the immense trust Queen Meridia had placed in their abilities. The energy shield represented their queen's mastery of magic and her determined belief in their collective strength.

As the shimmering waves of the shield enveloped the brave group, they could feel the pulsating energy resonating within their very beings. It was a powerful reminder that they were united, bound together by a common purpose and the unyielding support of their queen.

Zephyr, the revered elder and keeper of ancient wisdom, stepped forward, his eyes shimmering with the depth of his knowledge and experience. His voice resonated through the chamber, carrying the weight of countless generations and untold secrets. The room fell silent, captivated by his presence and eager to receive his final words of guidance.

"When the shadows grow deep, and your darkest fears begin to claw at your heart," Zephyr began, his voice a gentle yet commanding whisper, "when the clamor of doubts threatens to drown your resolve, it is in that pivotal moment that you must relinquish your attachments. Embrace the full spectrum of your being, including the depths of shame, failure, guilt, and darkness that reside within you. Do not resist their pull or futilely search for them; open yourself to their presence and acknowledge their existence."

The air in the room seemed to grow heavy as

Zephyr's words sank deep into the hearts of the brave merfolk. His wisdom resonated with them, for they understood the significance of his message. The path they were about to embark upon would test their spirits and challenge their essence. It was not merely a physical journey but a voyage into the depths of their souls.

"In accepting your fears, embracing them without judgment or condemnation, you shall discover the unexpected treasure that lies hidden within," Zephyr continued, his voice carrying a profound reverence. "For it is through the crucible of darkness that true transformation takes place. Embrace your shadows, my merfolk heroes, for within them lies the key to your liberation and the awakening of your hidden potential."

As Zephyr's words echoed in the room, the merfolk stood in awe, their hearts filled with trepidation and ignited with a newfound determination. They understood that their journey was not solely about unraveling the secrets of the rock and the Eternal City but also about delving deep into the recesses of their own beings. It was a pilgrimage of self-discovery, where their darkest fears would be confronted and transmuted into sources of strength and enlightenment.

With a final nod of encouragement from Zephyr, the merfolk heroes embraced the weight of his wisdom, knowing that it would guide them through the awaiting trials. They could feel the tendrils of their own shadows intertwining with the shimmering hope that burned within their souls. The moment had come to embark on their transformative odyssey, armed with Zephyr's guidance and the unwavering support of their kingdom.

As they set forth, their collective resolve radiated like a beacon, drawing strength from each other and the profound insights bestowed upon them. The echoes of Zephyr's words resonated within their hearts, reminding them that true glory awaited those who dared to face their innermost fears. With each step they took, they embraced the journey that would unravel the secrets of the rock and the Eternal City and the mysteries that lay dormant within their own beings.

.Ten.
Bistro Mosa

10

The door swung open, releasing a gentle creak that mingled with the ambient sounds of Bistro Mosa. Kairos, a figure of elegance and mystery, confidently crossed the threshold. Sheila, the establishment's proprietor, greeted him with genuine excitement, her eyes sparkling with warmth and curiosity.

"Kairos, it's been a while. Where have your journeys taken you?" she exclaimed, unable to contain her delight. "You possess a timeless charm that defies the passage of time."

Kairos' enigmatic smile played across his lips as he responded, his voice conveying intrigue. "My dear Sheila, I've ventured to distant lands, exploring the realms where mythical herbs bloom and ancient wisdom thrives. In these hidden corners of the world, I seek the secrets of healing and transformation."

Sheila's eyes widened with fascination, captivated by the allure of Kairos' exotic pursuits. "Your travels are as enchanting as ever," she murmured, her voice filled with admiration. "Tell me, what wondrous discoveries have you made on your latest odyssey?"

Kairos' gaze grew distant as he recounted his exploits, his words carrying the weight of countless untold stories. "In the valleys of the Himalayas, I encountered a rare flower said to hold the essence of eternal youth. In the depths of the Amazon rainforest, I communed with ancient spirits who revealed the hidden properties of sacred plants. And among the rolling hills of Ireland, I unraveled the mysteries of an herb said to possess the power to mend a broken heart."

Sheila's eyes widened in awe, her imagination whisked away by the vivid tapestry of Kairos' adventures. "Your knowledge and expertise are truly extraordinary," she whispered, her voice laced with reverence. "You are a guardian of nature's secrets, a bridge between the realms of myth and reality."

Kairos chuckled softly, his eyes gleaming with humility and pride. "I am but a humble servant of the natural world, weaving the threads of ancient wisdom into potions and elixirs that bring solace and restoration. It is a calling I am honored to pursue."

Their conversation carried a sense of timeless camaraderie, as though they had traversed many lifetimes together. The air in Bistro Mosa became infused with an aura of magic and possibility as they exchanged stories of mythical herbs, transformative journeys, and the profound impact of their shared passions.

"How is Hank doing?" Kairos asked, his voice tinged with genuine concern. His eyes, filled with a mix of compassion, searched Sheila's face for any glimmer of hope.

Sheila's expression softened, her eyes reflecting the weight of the situation. "Hank's state has worsened since he claimed to have encountered the unicorns," she replied, her voice laced with empathy. "The allure and mystery of these mythical beings have ensnared his mind, entwining his thoughts in a labyrinth of obsession. His once-promising career has been shattered, and he has become the subject of ridicule among his colleagues. It pains me to see him suffer like this. "

Kairos nodded, understanding the gravity of the situation. His eyes, filled with compassion, met Sheila's gaze.

"If anyone can help Hank find his way back from the depths of despair, it is you, Kairos," she said, her voice tinged with gratitude. "His boat, anchored far from the shores, has become his sanctuary and prison. We must find a way to reach him so that he may regain his sanity and reclaim his rightful place among the esteemed academics."

The door swung open again, and a group of weary youths shuffled into Bistro Mosa. Their shoulders slumped with exhaustion, and disappointment lingered in their eyes. Sensing their downtrodden spirits, Sheila, the warm and welcoming hostess, approached them with a gentle smile.

"Welcome, my young friends," she said, her voice brimming with compassion. "How can I help you today?"

Drew mumbled softly, "We were looking for unicorns... but they seem to exist only in stories."

Giselle chimed in, her voice filled with a mixture of longing and resignation, "Perhaps a refreshing drink could lift our spirits?"

Sheila's smile grew wider as she sensed an opportunity to bring some joy into their lives. "Ah, you've come to the right place," she replied, her eyes twinkling mischievously. "We have a special blend that may just do the trick. It's created by none other than the legendary herbal alchemist, Kairos, who happens to be here today."

The mention of Kairos piqued the teens' curiosity, and their tired eyes lit up with a glimmer of hope. Just as though summoned by their conversation, Kairos emerged from the depths of the bistro, his presence exuding an aura of wisdom and intrigue. With a graceful stride, he approached the table, a knowing smile dancing upon his lips.

"Why were you so upset, my young friends?" he inquired, his voice laced with genuine concern.

The teenagers exchanged glances, unsure of where to begin. They had been on a relentless quest to find the unicorns and uncover the truth about Hank Kahawai. Still, everywhere they went, they were met with mockery and disbelief whenever they brought up these subjects. The weight of their disappointment and society's disbelief made it difficult for them to find the words to express their frustration.

To everyone's surprise, Fergus, who slept most of the time and had never spoken in public before, lifted his head, his eyes ablaze with newfound determination. Once timid and uncertain, his voice now carried a firmness that commanded attention.

"We read an old newspaper about Hank Kahawai and his encounter with unicorns," he announced, each word punctuated with conviction. "We would like to meet him in person."

The gang was taken aback by Fergus's change. It was like a slumbering ember had been fanned into a roaring flame, igniting his spirit with purpose.

Kairos, his eyes gleaming with curiosity and ancient wisdom, leaned in closer, his gaze fixed on Fergus. "You've looked into the story of Hank Kahawai?" he inquired, his voice tinged with intrigue. "Tell me more, young seeker."

"It spoke of Hank's extraordinary bond with the unicorns near the Marian Trench and how their graceful presence had forever altered his perception of reality." Fergus recounted, his voice steady and resolute.

Kairos's lips curled into a knowing smile, a flicker of ancient recognition dancing in his eyes. "I, too, have been searching for Hank," he confessed, his voice laced with a quiet sense of purpose. "It appears that our paths have converged, entwined by the threads of fate and the allure of the unknown."

Lily, her eyes wide with wonder, couldn't help but interject, her voice filled with longing and curiosity. "Do you believe in unicorns and magic, Kairos?" she asked, her words filled with both skepticism and a glimmer of hope.

Sheila, returning with a tray of drinks, overheard the teenagers' conversation and couldn't help but interject. Her tone carried a mix of concern and weariness.

"No, not again," she exclaimed, a hint of dismay lacing her words. "Another group caught in the frenzy of unicorn tales. But perhaps you're asking the right person. Kairos is a manifestation of magic; perhaps after you've finished these drinks, you'll understand."

A knowing smile played upon Kairos's lips as he regarded Lily with eyes that seemed to hold the wisdom of ages. His voice resonated with a depth that commanded attention.

"Belief is a peculiar concept," he responded, his words carrying the weight of countless legends and untold stories. "To me, the line between belief and reality blurs, for life itself is a tapestry woven with magic. It manifests itself in whispers of belief and unexplained synchronicities, in the graceful dance of universe and the enigmatic mysteries hidden within the depths of nature."

The group couldn't help but be drawn into Kairos's words, their thoughts swirling with wonder and curiosity.

Yet amidst the contemplation, Wild interjected, his tone laced with humor. "That's some deep philosophy you've got there. Maybe these drinks will hold the key to unlocking the magic," he quipped, raising his glass in a playful toast. With a mischievous grin, he downed the drink in a single, confident gulp, his companions following suit.

As the drink caressed their tongues, subtle energy seemed to permeate the air, casting a hushed enchantment upon the room. The flavors mingled in a symphony of familiar and exotic tastes, infusing the teenagers with a sense of intrigue and anticipation. A gentle warmth spread through their bodies, a feeling that whispered of hidden possibilities and the promise of adventure.

Giselle's eyes shimmered with newfound curiosity as she turned to Kairos, her gaze filled with a radiant mix of awe and intrigue. A genuine smile bloomed on her lips, reflecting the profound impact of her experience. Her voice, laced with wonder and excitement, expressed her profound realization.

"Kairos, you are a true alchemist," she acknowledged, her voice filled with marvel. "The moment I took a sip, a wave of tranquility and joy washed over me. All my exhaustion and frustration from the previous few weeks vanished."

Giselle grinned and took another sip of her drink. "These drinks contain something extraordinary, seem a portal that opens my mind to the world's mysteries. It's as if a veil has been lifted, revealing the hidden enchantment surrounding us," she went on.

Kairos chuckled softly, his laughter resonating with a touch of amusement. He enjoyed observing the young ones as they wholeheartedly embraced the magic that enveloped them. "Indeed," he responded, his voice carrying a soothing warmth.

"Sometimes, a mere sip of the extraordinary can awaken our senses to the wonders surrounding us. However, remember that the true essence of magic lies not solely in the elixir or anything outside of you, but rather in the journey you embark upon, the profound discoveries you make, and the meaningful connections you forge along the way."

The Dreamy Dreamy

"Wait," Drew exclaimed, his voice filled with excitement. "This is the dreamy dreamy that my grandmother used to make for me."

G.T. scratched his head, a perplexed expression forming on his face. His brows furrowed as he struggled to make sense of the situation. "Your grandma?" he stammered, his confusion evident. "I thought you were raised by a black jaguar."

Drew let out a small sigh and shook his head, clarifying, "No, no. She's not an actual jaguar. She has a deep connection with the spirit of the black jaguar, embodying its strength and wisdom."

Kairos, his eyes gleaming with recognition, focused his gaze on Drew. A smile of familiarity graced his face, and he nodded in affirmation. "Yes, Drew, you are that kid," he acknowledged, his voice filled with fond reminiscence.

"I remember vividly working alongside your extraordinary grandmother deep within the heart of the Amazon forest. She was a revered shaman, a guardian of ancient wisdom and mystical traditions. Her connection to the spirit of the black jaguar was awe-inspiring, as she embodied its strength and harnessed its boundless wisdom. She bestowed upon me the sacred knowledge of the dreamy dreamy remedy. This potion transcends the realms of dreams and reveals the hidden depths of our souls."

Drew's eyes widened in astonishment, his mind struggling to process the profound revelation. "You know my grandma?" he exclaimed, a mix of shock and awe resonating in his voice. Kairos nodded with a warm smile, a glimmer of shared memories flickering in his eyes.

Wild raised his hands in frustration, unable to conceal the perplexity. "What exactly is going on here?" Grandma? "Black Jaguar?" he said, his voice hazy with confusion and curiosity.

The group turned their attention to Sara, who had assumed the role of the spiritually knowledgeable sage, sensing the need to shed light on the enigmatic puzzle that unfolded before them.

Sara cleared her throat and began to explain the intricacies of Drew's ancestral lineage. "You see," she began, her voice filled with reverence, "Drew's family carries a sacred lineage of shamans who profoundly understand the natural world and its hidden realms. They can transcend the boundaries of ordinary existence through their connection with animal spirits and mastery of energy and forms. Drew's grandmother, though not a literal black jaguar, embodies the essence and teachings of this majestic creature. However, some claimed they could literally transform into animals. It's called 'shapeshifting.'"

A sense of awe settled over the group, their minds trying to grasp the depth of Drew's heritage and its implications for their journey.

Kairos' gaze encompassing the room, he continued soothingly, "This gathering, my friends, is no coincidence. We have been brought together by the threads of fate, drawn to this moment where the lines between reality and magic blur. Drew's lineage, the unicorns, and Hank's encounter are all intertwined, each playing a pivotal role in the unfolding puzzles of our shared destiny."

Giselle, her eyes wide with anticipation, leaned forward, her curiosity palpable. "So, what do we do next? How are we going to find Hank?" she inquired, her voice filled with excitement and determination.

Kairos, his gaze filled with compassion, acknowledged their eagerness. "Now, my young friends," he began, his voice carrying a soothing resonance, "you all need to have a good rest. It is essential to immerse yourselves in the magic of the dreamy dreamy." A caring smile graced his lips as he continued, "Sometimes, when one feels lost or overwhelmed, it is always good to delve into the realms of dreams and recharge the body. In the dreamland where the boundaries between the seen and the unseen blur, we can commune with spirits, seek guidance from ancient wisdom, and unlock the profound mysteries that await us."

Sheila, the ever-attentive hostess, stepped forward, her eyes filled with concern. "Before you embark on your dream-filled journey, where will you stay on the island?" she inquired.

G.T.'s eyes widened as he realized their oversight. "Oh no, we forgot to book a guest house," he muttered, a touch of worry in his voice.

Sheila, quick on her feet, offered a solution. "How about our Moonstar cottage near the coast?" she suggested, a glimmer of excitement in her eyes. "It's currently vacant and would be the perfect sanctuary for your mystical quest."

"That's awesome!" The gang erupted in cheers, grateful for the serendipitous turn of events.

With a profound understanding of the unfolding events, Kairos exchanged a knowing look with Sheila. "It is about time," he mused, his voice carrying a hint of anticipation. His gaze shifted to the unusual necklace adorning his neck, its intricate carvings depicting mesmerizing orbits of galaxies instead of a conventional clock.

"Rest well, my dear friends. We shall meet again soon," he declared, his words imbued with assurance and mystery.

As the teenagers made their way to the Moonstar cottage, their hearts filled with anticipation and the promise of enchanting dreams, they couldn't help but wonder what awaited them on this extraordinary journey. Little did they know that their dreams would be woven with threads of ancient wisdom, guiding them closer to the enigmatic Hank Kahawai and the elusive unicorns they sought.

Before Dawn

A solitary figure emerged from the darkness as the vivid hues of the stunning daybreak began to paint the sky, casting an enchanting shine upon the serene surroundings. Hank, once a promising marine biologist, now a scruffy young man, had already begun his laborious chores before dawn. He worked hard, oblivious to the world around him, motivated by a sense of purpose that appeared to absorb his every thought.

In this early hour, as the world awakened, Kairos approached Hank with a sense of determination. "It's been a while!" His voice cut through the stillness, carrying a touch of hurry.

Startled, Hank paused his work, his weary eyes meeting Kairos's gaze. A mix of weariness and curiosity lingered in his expression as he asked, "What brings you here?" His voice held a tinge of detachment, hinting at the depths of his contemplation and the weight of his responsibilities.

Undeterred by Hank's initial indifference, Kairos pressed on, his eyes filled with concern and curiosity. "Do you mind if I come aboard?" he asked, seeking permission to join Hank on the boat.

Hank shook his head in a gesture of acquiescence, silently granting Kairos access to the deck. Finding a cozy spot, Kairos settled himself, ready to engage in conversation.

"How is your research progressing, Hank?" Kairos inquired, his tone filled with genuine interest.

Yet, Hank remained silent, focused on his tasks, seemingly unable or unwilling to divert his attention.

Undeterred by the lack of response, Kairos continued, his voice laced with unrelenting drive. "Are you still searching for the elusive unicorns?" he probed, hoping to evoke a deeper connection.

Hank's hands stilled at that moment, and he turned his gaze toward Kairos. There was a flicker of something in his eyes, a glimmer of unspoken words yearning to be expressed. But just as quickly, he resumed his work, the unfinished thoughts lingering.

Kairos persisted, his relentless determination evident in his next question. "Have you had the chance to read TiTi's letter?" he inquired, his voice filled with urgency.

Hank's reluctant response betrayed a mixture of curiosity and reluctance. "No," he admitted, his voice tinged with regret. Yet, as though struck by a sudden realization, a spark of recognition illuminated Hank's face. "TiTi... it's the necklace! It's the necklace!" he exclaimed, a sense of urgency propelling him into action. Without further delay, he hurriedly exited the boat, gratitude evident in his words. "Thank you, Kairos! I need to return to the cottage immediately."

Moonstar Cottage

As the velvety night embraced the Moonstar cottage, its tranquil walls cradled Lily and her friends, who had sought refuge in its mystical embrace. Under the enchanting moonlight, they surrendered themselves to the transformative power of the dreamy dreamy, each embarking on their own profound journey within the realm of dreams.

And as the first tendrils of sunlight delicately caressed the horizon, the cottage awakened with a subtle shimmer, its essence radiating an enchanting aura. The interplay of light and shadow danced upon the walls, casting mesmerizing patterns that seemed to ripple and sway with a life of their own. The cottage was seemingly alive, pulsating with a mysterious energy that whispered of forgotten enchantments.

In this magical awakening, Lily, the sole early riser, felt an inexplicable pull, an irresistible invitation from the heart of the cottage. Curiosity ignited within her, urging her to embark on a solitary exploration, her footsteps light and filled with anticipation. The house seemed to beckon her forward, its secrets waiting to be unveiled.

Lily's eyes widened in astonishment as she entered the parlor, taking in the extensive collection of books and the life aura that permeated the area. The air crackled with gentle energy as though the knowledge contained within the weathered pages had taken on a life of its own, ready to impart its secrets to those willing to listen. Ancient wisdom seemed to whisper from the shelves, guiding her gaze to the most intriguing volumes and inviting her to delve into their mystical pages.

But the true enchantment awaited beyond the threshold of the main house. The enchanting garden, bathed in the morning light, called to Lily with its vibrant lives of flora. Each step she took along its winding paths was met with a symphony of scents and colors, just like the flowers sought to captivate her senses. Delicate petals unfurled like celestial dancers, their hues and fragrances blending harmoniously. The whispering breeze carried a symphony of voices feeling like the flora and fauna were engaged in an ancient conversation known only to nature.

In the heart of the garden, a small clearing revealed a mesmerizing sight—a shimmering fountain, its waters imbued with a subtle luminescence that cast a soft, otherworldly glow. Droplets whirled in the air, catching the morning light and spreading it in a rainbow of colors. Lily felt a gentle pull toward the fountain's edge as though it held the key to unlock the mysteries of the universe. She cupped her hands, allowing the water to cascade through her fingers, feeling its cool touch imbue her with a sense of harmony and serenity.

But the allure of the silent forest beckoned irresistibly. As Lily ventured deeper into its verdant depths, a hushed reverence settled upon her. Ancient trees towered above, their branches intertwined like mystical tapestries woven by unseen hands. Shafts of sunlight pierced through the canopy, casting ethereal rays that danced upon the forest floor. The air seemed to vibrate with palpable energy as if the very essence of nature whispered ancient secrets in every rustle of leaves.

And there it stood, concealed amidst the verdant embrace—the crown Jewell of the silent forest, the magnificent 'Rainbow Waterfall'. As Lily approached, a sense of wonder enveloped her being. The waterfall cascaded down with heavenly grace, each droplet glistening with the colors of the spectrum. The water seemed to possess a captivating song, its melodic rhythm enchanting all who stood in its presence. A gentle mist enveloped the surroundings, carrying with it the whispers of dreams and the promises of newfound understanding.

In this mystical haven of the Moonstar cottage, Lily found herself transported to a realm where reality intertwined with the magical. Time seemed to lose its grip as she immersed herself in the timeless charm of the cottage and its captivating surroundings. Here, dreams were nurtured, wisdom was discovered, and the world's wonders were unveiled in all their mystical splendor.

☆

On the other side, a profound silence encased the air in a cocoon of serenity as the magnificent golden glow of dawn flooded over the Moonstar cottage. The members of the gang awoke one by one, their thoughts pulsing with transcendent clarity and a deep sense of awareness. Their dreamscapes remained entwined with the fabric of reality, building a web of profound insight and boundless illumination.

The tranquil ambiance was disrupted by Wild's exclamation of surprise as a handsome young man with his hair tied up walked into the room. "I thought we were the only ones staying here," he exclaimed, his eyes wide with astonishment.

With her just-woken-up appearance, Giselle brushed past Wild and calmly replied, "That's Fergus. Come on, don't be startled."

Wild, now vigilant, approached Fergus with a mix of curiosity and recognition. "Fergus, it's really you! I've never seen your face clearly until now," he exclaimed, his excitement palpable.

Fergus smiled, emanating quiet confidence from within.

Meanwhile, Sara and G.T. had found themselves immersed in the collection of books in the parlor, their attention momentarily diverted by the commotion. They turned their focus to Fergus and exclaimed in unison, "Fergus!" Their voices echoed with surprise and intrigue, their eyes widening with anticipation.

Sara couldn't contain her curiosity any longer and blurted out, "Why did you always cover your pretty face with your hair?

Fergus hesitated momentarily, contemplating

how to put his thoughts into words. "Well," he began, "I see things differently."

Wild furrowed his brow and asked, "What do you mean?"

Fergus took a deep breath and gathered his thoughts before continuing. "I can see people's auras and the secrets hidden within them," he admitted, his gaze steadfast.

Sara couldn't help but interject excitedly, "You're clairvoyant!"

Fergus nodded in response to her remark. "I've had this gift since I was a kid. It puzzled me because I could always tell when people were lying." He took a break to rearrange his thoughts. "When their words and feelings were at odds, I knew instantly. But I didn't know whether to play along or reveal it. So I went into hiding, covered my face, and pretended to sleep."

Fergus glanced at the gathering with deep, pure blue eyes that seemed to pierce the depths of their souls. The intensity of his gaze conveyed a profound understanding and empathy like he could perceive the innermost thoughts and emotions of each person before him. The gathering listened closely, their interest growing with each syllable from Fergus's mouth.

G.T. couldn't help himself asking, "Then why did you stop disguising?"

Fergus paused in response, a sweet smile on his lips. It was a smile that radiated wisdom and acceptance, a monument to the growth he had undergone on his journey. "I believe the cottage and the dreamy dreamy worked their magic on me," he said, his voice resonating with newfound peace.

"When I woke up this morning, I had a moment of epiphany. People lie for various reasons, and it is not my place to criticize or untangle the complexities of their lives. Perhaps they aren't yet ready to face the truth, or their circumstances don't allow complete honesty."

Fergus' words hung in the air like a gentle embrace of understanding and sympathy. His insight emphasized the significance of respect and empathy when navigating the intricacy of human nature. "I realized that my gift, the ability to see beyond the surface, grants me glimpses of their lives but never the entire expanse," he added, his voice filled with profound modesty.

"As a result, I decided to drop the desire to reveal or pretend. Instead, I accept the role of an observer, respecting others' decisions and journeys, recognizing that true understanding rests not in uncovering their secrets, but in accepting and supporting them on their own paths."

The resonance of Fergus's remarks reverberated across the room as they lingered in the air. Each person was deeply moved by his inspirational insight, which stirred feelings of compassion and understanding. He revealed to them the fundamental value of respect and compassion in navigating the complex web of human nature, and the weight of his discovery settled upon them.

As Fergus spoke, the room seemed to be enveloped in hushed reverence, almost like the very walls of the Moonstar cottage absorbed his wisdom. The gang exchanged glances, their eyes reflecting a newfound appreciation for the complexities of life and the beauty that lies in accepting others as they are.

"Good morning, guys," Drew entered the parlor with a warm greeting.

The group acknowledged the salutation, their attention immediately captured by Drew's unexpected appearance.

Wild's eyes widened with astonishment as he blurted out, "Wait a second! Why are you dressed like a girl?"

Sara looked at Wild with an amused glint and couldn't help but giggle at his mystified appearance.

Sara declared, teasing Wild, "She is a girl all the time."

Wild's mind was still spinning from Fergus' revelations as he shook his head in disbelief. "No, not twice. Is today's game an undercover one?" he shouted, his tone a mix of uncertainty and amazement. He felt like he had entered a whimsical world where identities and secrets continually changed due to the morning's unanticipated turns.

☆

Drew found a comfortable position on the sofa, crossed her legs, and relaxedly leaned back.

"Actually, my name is Jewell, not Drew," she said with a nostalgic tone.

The group eagerly drew in to hear her story as the room slipped into a weird quiet.

"It's a long story," Jewell said. "When I was little, my grandmother raised me. My parents were city workers, and one day my father came to find a picture of me cuddling a black jaguar in a local newspaper. He worried the jaguar might hurt me as he wasn't familiar with shaman practices."

G.T., listening attentively to Jewell's story, suddenly had a thoughtful expression. As he assimilated the facts, he had an epiphany. "So that's why people always joked about you, Jewell, saying you were raised by a black jaguar?" he asked, his voice packed with interest and empathy.

His statements conveyed a newfound awareness of Jewell's background and pity for the misunderstandings she had experienced. The group sat silent as they recognized the deeper levels of Jewell's narrative and its weight.

Jewell chuckled, a twinkle of amusement in her eyes. "Yes, the rumors spread like wildfire, becoming an ongoing joke. Little did they know that my connection with the black jaguar was more than just a playful jest. It embodied the ancient shamanic lineage that runs through my family."

Jewell took a moment to let her words sink in before moving on. "You see, the female characters in my family were the ones who carried along the shamanic heritage. In his naivety, my father thought that if I pretended to be a boy, I would be protected from the black jaguar's influence. I gradually lost sight of who I really was because he depicted shamans as nothing more than primitive charlatans."

As Jewell described her journey of self-discovery, the atmosphere in the room was palpably charged with curiosity and empathy. Wild, who was still trying to make sense of the incredible happenings of the day, found a seat and sat down since he needed some time to gather his thoughts.

"This is only getting crazier today! His voice was filled with astonishment and humor as he remarked, "I need to sit down. I guess the dreamy dreamy has also had an effect on you."

Jewell nodded in accord, a warm smile spreading across her face. "Indeed, after drinking the dreamy dreamy yesterday, I got bogged down with memories of my grandmother. I started to think about all the people who had turned to her in the past for help and guidance. They carried heartfelt gratitude and frequently shed tears. Nothing resembled the twisted picture my father had given me. And last night, in my dream, a black jaguar showed up as if to lead me back to my true path," Jewell revealed, her voice carrying a profound awakening.

Her words carried the essence of timeless wisdom, spreading in the air. It appeared as though the walls whispered empowering and self-discovery-related secrets as the room glistened with a fresh luminosity. A gentle breeze rustled through the cottage, carrying the delicate fragrance of blooming flowers as an offering from the unseen forces that embraced Jewell's journey.

"I realized that the black jaguar's presence in my dream was more than a mere vision," Jewell continued, her voice firmer with conviction. "She was guiding me back to my true nature, urging me to honor the essence within me, no matter what others may think. We all carry the threads of our ancestral lineage, yet, it is our birthright to craft our own path and explore the depths of our individual nature. There is no use in resisting it because the ultimate liberty comes from embracing our authentic selves."

As Jewell spoke, the air in the room seemed to vibrate with newfound energy. Shadows danced on the walls, casting ancient symbols and glyphs that pulsed with an otherworldly light. Their hearts stirred by Jewell's words, and the group felt a resonance deep within their souls. It was like the cottage embraced their individuality, encouraging them to venture into the uncharted territories of their dreams and aspirations.

Outside, the surrounding nature seemed to respond to the unfolding tale. Birds sang a harmonious chorus, their notes harmonizing with the rhythm of Jewell's voice. The wind whispered secrets, carrying echoes of forgotten chants and enchantments. Even the gentle rustling of leaves became melodic, seemingly like the very trees were lending their voices to the unfolding narrative.

In the enchanting haven of the Moonstar cottage, where reality merged with the realms of magic and introspection, they understood that their journey was not merely a quest for answers but a celebration of their uniqueness. With renewed purpose, they pledged to honor their ancestral lineage while fearlessly forging their destinies, guided by the wisdom within and the unseen forces that whispered secrets in the wind.

After hearing Fergus and Jewell's profound revelations and feeling the mystical energy pulsating through the Moonstar cottage, Wild couldn't help but mumble, "I need a Zen moment to let all of this sink in. What exactly has this cottage done to us?" The weight of the revelations and the unfolding magic had left him both exhilarated and contemplative.

Sara couldn't help but chuckle, her voice reverberating across the room. "Aren't these why we came to this island? Seeking for mysteries and wonders?" With a sly gleam in her eyes, she teased.

The group joined in Sara's laughter, their spirits buoyed by the shared camaraderie and the realization that they were experiencing something extraordinary. The Moonstar cottage had become more than just a physical space—it was a vessel for transformation, a conduit through which their latent powers and desires were awakened.

"Hey guys, come look at this!" Giselle exclaimed,

her eyes widening with excitement as she uncovered a hidden treasure beneath the miscellaneous papers on the table.

The gang gathered around, their curiosity piqued. There, resting upon the table, was a wood necklace adorned with a small rough rock nestled at its center. Its earthy hues contrast against the polished wood. Like ancient whispers, intricate patterns were masterfully carved into the aged surface, telling a tale of forgotten lore. The necklace was meticulously secured with braided animal leather, each strand a testament to the craftsmanship that went into its creation.

"I've never seen patterns like these before," Sara remarked, her fingertips delicately tracing the intricate engravings. "The symbols seemed to hold a mystical energy."

G.T. leaned in closer, his eyes squinting to decipher the cryptic symbols etched on the back of the wooden frame. "There's more to this necklace than it appears," he murmured, his voice filled with intrigue and fascination.

The air in the room crackled with an otherworldly aura as though the necklace itself held a secret longing to be unraveled.

"Look," G.T. continued, his eyes narrowing as he

examined the necklace closely. He pointed to the symbols engraved on the back of the wooden frame. "These symbols seem to hold significance. They look ancient, possibly representing a forgotten language or a secret message."

As Giselle pondered the purpose of the small rough rock at the center of the necklace, a sense of wonder filled the room. "Why did they put this seemingly ordinary rock in it instead of a sparkling gem or a lustrous pearl?" she speculated, her gaze fixed on the curious stone. The gang exchanged intrigued glances, their minds filled with questions and curiosity.

☆

Unbeknownst to them, the necklace had a story beyond mere aesthetics. It held a hidden power, a connection to a forgotten realm of magic and ancient wisdom. The rock, although unassuming in appearance, contained within it the essence of the earth, carrying the energy of ancient lands and long-lost civilizations. Its rough surface held the whispers of untold tales and untapped potential.

G.T., driven by his insatiable curiosity, reached out to touch the stone, his fingertips gently brushing against the rough surfaces. A faint tremor coursed through his hand as if the stone had responded to his touch. The room fell silent as the gang held their breath, captivated by the unfolding mystery.

"What are you doing here?" A sudden interruption shattered their fascination as the group marveled at the intricacies of the necklace. A scruffy man burst into the room, his disheveled appearance contrasting sharply with the aura of mystery that permeated the Moonstar cottage.

His stare was filled with urgency and longing as he focused on the necklace in G.T.'s hands. G.T. was startled and dropped the chain, which the strange man quickly picked up. "It's my necklace," he said, his voice full of anxiety and perplexity.

"Sheila brought us here," Fergus interjected, his voice steady and unyielding.

"Sheila?" The stranger's brow furrowed as he attempted to piece together the puzzle before him. The room became heavy with indescribable tension, leaving everyone uncertain how to respond.

Amid the uncertainty and tension in the air, the celestial melody weaved its way through the room, breaking through the walls of skepticism and doubt. Its ethereal notes wrapped around the room like a gentle embrace, casting a spell that seemed to transcend the boundaries of reality. As the enchanting melody unfolded, a wave of tranquility washed over the gang, dissolving the remnants of unease within them. The group exchanged bewildered glances, entranced by the otherworldly sound that seemed to beckon them forward.

"Who is singing?" the stranger asked, captivated by the alluring melody. Without hesitation, he made his way toward the door, his curiosity leading him to trace the source of the enchanting music.

Giselle spoke with certainty, her voice tinged with excitement, "That must be Lily. Let's follow."

Eager to uncover the source of the captivating melody, the gang followed the stranger as he walked past the enchanting garden and ventured deeper into the Silent Forest. Each step brought them closer to an awe-inspiring sight that left them breathless.

The stranger abruptly halted, and the group came to a standstill, their eyes widening in astonishment. Before them lay a magnificent scene straight out of a fantastical tale. A colossal waterfall cascaded down from great heights, its waters shimmering in the sunlight. As the rays of light kissed the rushing water, a mesmerizing display of multiple rainbows unfolded, layering the air with vibrant hues that danced and intertwined.

The surrounding trees became adorned with colorful birds perched upon their branches, singing perfectly harmoniously with Lily's heavenly voice. Butterflies and dragonflies fluttered gracefully around them, their delicate wings painting the air with a kaleidoscope of colors. Enchanted by the gentle breeze, flowers swayed and twirled in a mesmerizing dance.

But the magic didn't end there. In the crystal-clear waters below the waterfall, an orchestra of life unfolded. Various fishes, adorned with scales that shimmered like precious gems, gracefully swam, their movements synchronized with the enchanting melody. Frogs and cicadas joined in, creating a symphony of quacks and chirps that intertwined seamlessly with the otherworldly music.

The waterfall seemed alive, responding to the melody with a dance. It leaped and twirled, the water glistening as it flowed down in a mesmerizing rhythm mirroring the enchanting song that filled the forest. It was a harmonious convergence of nature's elements orchestrated by unseen hands.

The gang stood in awe, their hearts overflowing with wonder. They had entered a realm where nature and music merged into a breathtaking symphony of sights and sounds. It was a magical moment that seemed to exist outside the confines of time and space, where the boundaries between reality and dreams blurred into a seamless tapestry of enchantment.

They embraced the magical scene before them with wide-eyed amazement and joyful hearts. They couldn't help but feel that they were on the cusp of a profound journey, where the melody, the forest, and their destinies intertwined in ways they were yet to comprehend. And as they stood in the presence of nature's orchestra, they couldn't wait to delve deeper into the secrets that awaited them in this mystical realm.

Lily was lost in her world of music, inattention to the crowd that had silently gathered behind her. She took a graceful bow as gratitude for the magnificent display of nature's symphony filled her eyes. Lily turned around with a contented smile, quickly replaced by shock and confusion as realizing that everyone was looking at her. She smiled and said, "I was unaware of you guys," but her demeanor had a tinge of shyness.

"Where did you pick up this song?" A surge of curiosity consumed the stranger, urging him to uncover the origins of the enchanting melody. His voice resonated with wonder and longing as he posed his question to Lily.

Startled by the unexpected attention, Lily turned her head, searching for the face that matched the inquisitive voice. The weight of the stranger's gaze unsettled her, causing her heart to flutter with nervous anticipation.

Summoning her inner strength, Lily steadied herself, drawing a deep breath that seemed to carry the weight of her childhood dreams. With trepidation, she revealed her ethereal connection with the captivating song. Her words unfurled with deliberate precision, each syllable carrying the weight of years spent harboring a secret longing.

"This melody has been in my dreams since I was a child," she confessed, her voice trailing with a hint of wonder and mystery.

The stranger's eyes widened as Lily spoke, mirroring the astonishment that surged within him. His curiosity had unveiled a hidden world that resonated deep within Lily's soul. The stranger's face softened, his gaze filled with emotions. Something seemed to occupy his thoughts as a profound realization had washed over him. The cool breeze gently tousled the stranger's unkempt hair, accentuating the enigmatic aura surrounding him.

Their eyes locked, momentarily suspended in a moment of recognition. Lily stared at his face, now clearly visible to her, and a sense of familiarity washed over her like a distant memory resurfacing.

"You are... Professor Kahawai?" Lily's voice trembled slightly as she posed the question, her heart pounding with uncertainty and hope.

The stranger's eyes widened in surprise, a glimmer of astonishment dancing within them. "You know me?" he replied, his voice laced with disbelief.

"Professor Kahawai?" the gang exclaimed in unison, their voices filled with astonishment and curiosity. Now even more perplexed, Hank furrowed his brow, trying to make sense of the situation unfolding before him.

"We came here for you," Giselle said, her eyes sparkling excitedly.

The weight burdened the gang's shoulders seemed to dissipate instantly, replaced by a renewed sense of purpose and eagerness. They excitedly explained how they had stumbled upon Professor Kahawai's story, the inspiration it had ignited, and how they had traveled thousands of miles in pursuit of this serendipitous encounter.

Giselle's words hung in the air, carrying a profound sense of destiny and their paths intertwining. The forest seemed to crackle with energy as if the threads of fate had woven them together at this moment. Hank, his confusion slowly giving way to a glimmer of understanding, looked at the group with fascination and intrigue. The silence followed was fraught with expectation, with each gang member waiting for the professor's response with bated breath, unsure of what it might entail.

The melody that had danced through the air and touched the depths of Hank's soul had also managed to dissolve the guardedness that had encapsulated him for many years. It was a poignant moment for Hank as he reflected on the journey his life had taken since his story was released. Once hailed as a promising talent, he had faced ridicule and mockery that had stripped him of his confidence and shattered his dreams.

But here he was, surrounded by a group of young souls who had traveled thousands of miles to meet him, intrigued by his story and eager to embark on an adventure with him. Hank's lips curled up in a bittersweet smile at the absurdity of it all.

"I faced numerous challenges after my story went public." I lost my bright career and became a laughingstock. And now you're here seeking me out because of that story. Life's contradictions never cease to amaze me," he said, his voice tinged with vulnerability.

"You guys are insane," he chuckled, his disbelief transforming into a sense of exhilaration. With a gleam of excitement in his eye, Hank shared a daring idea that had ignited his adventurous spirit. "I'm going sailing this evening. Would you like to join?" he proposed, his voice brimming with contagious enthusiasm.

The gang erupted in cheers and enthusiastic affirmations. "Count us in!" they cried, their voices resonating excitedly.

With new hope rising in Hank's heart, he felt excitement and a renewed sense of purpose. The prospect of embarking on a sailing adventure with this spirited group filled him with anticipation and a longing for the unknown. It was a chance to leave behind the scars of the past and embrace the endless possibilities ahead.

As they cheered and celebrated, Fergus noticed Wild standing quietly by the waterfall, his gaze fixed on something hidden beneath its cascading waters. Concerned by his friend's uncharacteristic behavior, Fergus approached Wild and gently asked, "What happened, Wild?"

Wild turned to face Fergus, his eyes full of wonder and fascination. "I saw something under the waterfall," he replied, his voice filled with a hint of mystery.

Fergus's curiosity piqued, and he asked, "What is

it? What did you see?"

Wild paused for a moment as though debating whether or not to announce his discoveries. Then, he replied, "It's okay, never mind," flashing a comforting smile, "Let's go."

With a sense of unspoken understanding, Fergus nodded and followed Wild back to join the rest of the gang and Hank at the Moonstar cottage.

.Eleven.
The Void of Whispering

11

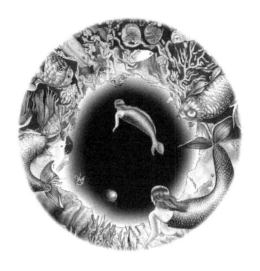

With the energy shield emanating a radiant glow, the merfolk heroes embarked on their journey toward the Void of Whispering. As they continued their voyage, the merfolk found themselves guided by the current itself, their path shaped by Evelina's profound affinity with the underwater currents.

She communed with the water's ebb and flow, conversing in a language known only to those who had delved into the ocean's deepest secrets and undergone years of training. The currents shared tales of ancient legends and whispered secrets of the sea, serving as a compass to guide the merfolk heroes along their path.

The ocean currents guided them through a labyrinth of underwater tunnels, where bioluminescent creatures illuminated their path with a dazzling display of colors. Schools of enchanted fish swam alongside them, their iridescent scales reflecting the shimmering magic that enveloped the group.

Suddenly, their keen senses detected a shift in their surroundings. The current's voice grew faint, and they entered a realm where its presence seemed to dissipate. A stillness washed over the waters, and an enchanting view unfolded before their eyes. It was a realm outside the boundaries of the Void of Whispering. This place seemed to seduce and entice explorers with its mythical allure.

"Look," Triton's voice echoed through the aquatic expanse, a mixture of awe and excitement lacing his words.

In this underwater marvel, something extraordinary caught the merfolk's attention. A flickering flame, akin to fire, danced upon the water's surface, defying the logic of the aquatic realm. It radiated a warm and vibrant glow, casting shimmering reflections upon the surrounding corals. The flame seemed to possess a life of its own, flickering and swaying with otherworldly energy.

Triton breathed, "This is way too bizarre," his eyes widening in wonder as he took in the captivating scene that had just been revealed to him.

An unexpected phenomenon occurred as the merfolk drew nearer to the flickering flame. A powerful suction force seemed to emanate from it, pulling them closer and closer until they were enveloped by the air-filled chamber. It was like the flame had opened a portal, allowing them to enter a world that defied the boundaries of their watery domain.

The transparent dome revealed a world untouched by water within the air-filled chamber. Lush vegetation sprouted from the ocean floor, forming a vibrant underwater forest that swayed with a gentle current. Exotic flowers, their petals adorned with iridescent hues, exuded intoxicating fragrances that wafted through the air, filling the space with an alluring scent.

But it wasn't just the flora that captivated the merfolk's attention. A symphony of ethereal melodies resounded through the chamber, carried by the gentle currents that danced among the air molecules. Harmonious voices sang in a language unknown to the merfolk, their enchanting tunes weaving tales of forgotten realms and lost legends.

"Where are we exactly?" Nadia's voice carried a blend of astonishment and curiosity as she drank in the exquisite scenery that unfolded before her.

The delicate snowflakes continued their descent, but instead of melting upon contact with the water, they remained suspended in the air, preserving their intricate crystalline structures. Each snowflake seemed to possess a unique design crafted with unparalleled precision. The merfolk reached out to touch them. As their fingertips grazed the frozen beauty, a tingling sensation coursed through their bodies, filling them with a profound sense of serenity and clarity.

In this extraordinary realm, time seemed to stand still, and the laws of the underwater world no longer applied. The flickering flame, the vibrant flora, the ethereal melodies, and the suspended snowflakes merged into a symphony of wonder and enchantment. It was a place where contradictions harmonized, fire and snow danced in perfect unison, reminding the merfolk of the infinite possibilities beyond their familiar realm's boundaries.

With their minds ablaze with curiosity and their spirits ignited by the fantastical scene, the merfolk heroes stepped forward, ready to venture deeper into the Void of Whispering. They carried the profound lessons and wondrous memories of the chamber of fire and snow, their hearts brimming with anticipation for the discoveries that awaited them in the depths of the whispering abyss.

The merfolk found themselves drawn towards the captivating sight, their curiosity ignited by the unknown wonders ahead. Yet, at that moment, Evelina's voice resonated through the depths, cautioning her companions of the risks that awaited them. She had received a transmission from the current, declaring that their escort had reached its end, and what lay beyond was a realm untouched by marine life.

The Haunting Fears

Amidst this breathtaking spectacle, the waters came alive with the presence of elusive beings. Radiant seashells, imbued with mysterious energy, gracefully glided through the water, their iridescent trails leaving a mesmerizing display in their wake. And there, among the ethereal dance of light and color, the

Void Spirits materialized.

These ethereal beings, known as Void Spirits, shimmered in translucent forms, their presence evoking a sense of ancient wisdom and tranquility. As they moved with a graceful fluidity, a sense of reverence filled the hearts of the merfolk. The Void Spirits possess an intimate understanding of the mysteries hidden beneath the void.

Veiled in an enigma air, the Void Spirits appeared as otherworldly guardians of the unknown. Their luminous forms glowed with an inner radiance, evoking a sense of the unseen wonders ahead. In their presence, there was a gentle reminder for all who approached this realm to be cautious, for the depths of the unknown held both mystery and danger.

Her eyes filled with caution and fascination, Evelina guided her companions through this enchanted realm. She urged them to maintain their focus and not be swayed by the allure of the mesmerizing creatures and vibrant landscapes.

"Remember," she reminded them, her voice carrying the weight of vigilance, "we are but visitors in this realm, and there are trials and tests that await us beyond the beauty we behold."

Triton, enticed by the irresistible beauty of the unknown, began to venture closer to the enchanting hole that beckoned them. However, Evelina swiftly called out to him, reminding the group that their true adventure was just beginning. She emphasized that the upcoming path would be fraught with challenges and tests, where they would need to confront their fears and overcome obstacles that lurked in the shadows.

Gathering all the merfolk around him, Orville raised his voice with conviction. "My dear merfolk, we stand on the precipice of the Void Nexus," he declared. "Where fears exist, it is where the greatest treasures are unveiled. Let us embrace our deepest fears and face them head-on, for within lies the path to our true potential and enlightenment. I have faith in each of you, and we shall emerge triumphant together."

As Orville spoke these words, a miraculous event occurred. The rock in his brood pouch emanated a radiant light, its brilliance pulsating in sync with his resolute words. The merfolk gazed in awe, their hearts filled with renewed confidence and determination. They understood that this was a sign, a tangible manifestation of their inner strength and the support that surrounded them.

The merfolk stepped forward one by one, entering the void with a determined will. The once enchanting sights dissolved into a veil of darkness as they passed through the chamber of fire and snow. Yet, instead of faltering, they pressed onward, guided by an unwavering belief in their capabilities.

Within the darkness, the merfolk faced their deepest fears. Shadows danced and twisted, whispering haunting melodies that threatened to unravel their resolve. But the merfolk, fueled by their shared determination, stood firm. They called upon their inner courage, their spirits refusing to be consumed by the darkness surrounding them.

As they traversed the void, the merfolk discovered a transformation within themselves. Each fear confronted, each obstacle overcome, ignited a spark of inner illumination. The darkness that had once seemed impenetrable began to fade, replaced by a flickering light that grew brighter with each step.

Undeterred, the merfolk pressed on, their perseverance unwavering. They swam closer together, seeking solace and strength in their shared presence. The flickering light that had guided them through the darkness continued to shine, providing a glimmer of hope amidst the encroaching Whispers.

But just as they thought they were on the verge of passing through the void, the merfolk found themselves engulfed in a heavy, inky blackness, their hearts pounding with uncertainty, and the flickering light suddenly went off. The absence of the guiding light left them momentarily disoriented, their senses heightened as they strained to perceive any sign of direction.

As the merfolk ventured deeper into the abyss, their confidence was bolstered by their progress. Yet, they couldn't ignore the growing intensity of the haunting whispers. The ghostly melodies echoed through the void, penetrating their very souls and stirring the embers of their deepest fears. The merfolk felt a chill creep up their spines, a palpable presence that refused to be ignored.

Orville observed with concern as some of his fellow merfolk displayed signs of distress. Despite their companions' soothing words and gestures of comfort, their unease was undeniable. The weight of the void pressed upon them, magnifying their insecurities and anxieties.

It was like the darkness sought to undermine their courage, whispering doubts into their ears and casting shadows upon their spirits. Each murmured reassurance from their companions seemed to lose its soothing touch, becoming a harsh reminder of their challenges. The merfolk's once-reliable support became a distorted reflection of their own fears, leaving them teetering on the precipice of doubt.

One by one, the merfolk felt the piercing sting of their fears, like knives sinking deep into their very beings. The more they resisted, the more profound their wounds became. The pain grew with each passing moment, threatening to engulf them in a sea of anguish. Some of the merfolk, overwhelmed by the intensity of their inner struggles, began to lose themselves in the vicious cycle of fear-fighting.

Despite their companions' encouragement and support, some merfolk succumbed to their doubts and insecurities. The weight of their apprehensions proved too burdensome, and with a heavy heart, they turned away from the path ahead. Their tails thrashed in a frantic retreat, desperate to escape the clutches of their own darkness.

Orville's gaze lingered upon those who had chosen to flee, a mix of sorrow and understanding etched upon his face. He knew that each merfolk's journey was unique, and not all were ready to face the depths of their innermost fears. While disappointment tugged at his heart, he respected their decision, for he understood that bravery cannot be forced—it must be embraced willingly.

Turning his attention back to the stalwart merfolk who remained, Orville drew upon the depths of his own fortitude. He spoke words that carried the weight of his experiences and the unwavering belief in their collective strength.

"We stand on the edge of shift," Orville's voice rang out, a beacon of resolve amidst the encroaching shadows. "Though the road ahead is challenging, and our fears threaten to consume us, we must remember that it is in the crucible of our deepest struggles that our true selves emerge. Let us raise our strength and confront our inner demons. Together, we shall prevail."

The merfolk, their hearts heavy with the departure of their companions, listened intently to Orville's impassioned words. Their determination ignited anew, a flicker of hope amidst the encircling darkness. They locked eyes, a silent pact forged in their shared resolve. They would confront their fears, not with reckless abandon, but with measured strength and unwavering support for one another.

"I'll lead the way," Triton, the fearless warrior, said with a firm voice, his eyes ablaze with determination. As one of the merfolk's most formidable protectors, Triton's unwavering commitment to the safety of his companions inspired courage in their hearts.

With synchronized strokes of their tails, the

merfolk resumed their advance into the heart of the void. The pain of their wounds persisted, each step a reminder of the battles waged within. But they refused to be consumed by their fears. They channeled their pain into determination, letting it fuel their decision to push forward.

The whispers of doubt and despair grew in intensity as the merfolk moved deeper into the abyss. Triton, the brave warrior who had taken the lead, was at the forefront of the onslaught. The malicious whispers twisted and distorted, aiming to awaken the darkest corners of his soul. The images of his fears appeared before him, encircling him like haunting ghosts.

The weight of guilt pressed upon Triton's heart as he relived the memories of his past. He saw himself as a helpless young boy, unable to protect his brother from the perils that befell them. The burden of his perceived failure had haunted him relentlessly throughout the years, despite his training to become a strong and resilient warrior. In his moments of vulnerability, the blame threatened to swallow his very essence.

Overwhelmed by the resurfacing pain, Triton's body seemed to shrink, his imposing figure diminishing into that of a sorrowful, crying child. His movements became hesitant, his once-fierce determination giving way to the overwhelming grip of his fears. The strong warrior now embodied the vulnerabilities and helplessness of that little boy he had once been.

While Triton found himself consumed by his fears, Nadia, swimming closely behind him, noticed his struggle and approached him, intending to offer assistance.

"Triton, are you alright?" Nadia spoke gently and concernedly to him. She had been observant of his demeanor throughout their journey, and now, as they faced the final challenges in the heart of The Void of Whispering, she could sense his inner turmoil.

However, as she drew nearer, an unforeseen transformation took place. Nadia's figure suddenly grew in size, her presence looming over Triton like a giant specter. Once gentle and comforting, her voice transformed into accusatory tones, blaming him for his perceived weaknesses and failures.

"I am sorry, so sorry, I couldn't save you from harm." Triton's heart sank as he watched Nadia's unexpected change. What was once his dear friend appeared as a haunting ghost, blaming him for things beyond his control. It was as if all his insecurities and doubts were given a terrifying form.

The rest of the group watched in shock as the situation unfolded. It became clear to them that this journey was one they needed to face individually, relying on their own inner strength and resilience. They understood that each merfolk had unique fears and challenges to confront. While support and camaraderie were vital, they ultimately had to face their inner demons alone.

With a heavy heart, Nadia realized the role she had unwittingly played in amplifying Triton's fears. She understood that her fears and insecurities had projected onto him, exacerbating his pain and inhibiting his ability to overcome his inner struggles. Moment of clarity, Nadia made the difficult decision to leave Triton's side, recognizing that he needed to face his fears without the added weight of her projections.

As Nadia swam away, her form returned to its original size. She rejoined the group. The merfolk, now more determined than ever, understood they had to rely on their inner strength and confront their deepest fears head-on. They rallied around Triton, offering silent support and understanding, but retrained from interfering in his personal battle. They recognized that their unity lay not in shielding each other from their fears but in standing together as individuals, each facing their own dark the ness with unwavering courage.

Nadia's realization weighed heavily on her, filling her with self-doubt and a sense of inadequacy. She blamed herself for not being good enough, believing that her actions had only brought harm to Triton. The negative emotions swirling within her became the nourishment for the whispers of fear, amplifying their power and reach. As she beat herself up, the haunting voices echoed her self-sabotage, intensifying the grip of fear around her.

"You did it again," she scolded herself, her mind a battleground of relentless blame. "Why couldn't you do it well? It turned out you caused more trouble for others. Why are you always like this?" The nonstop barrage of self-criticism engulfed her, drowning her in a sea of negativity.

During Nadia's inner turmoil, ever-perceptive Evelina sensed the distress in her fellow merfolk. She could hear the dialogue unfolding within Nadia's mind, filled with self-criticism and despair. Evelina felt deep compassion for Nadia's struggle and decided to Intervene, hoping to transmit supportive energy through her intention.

However, as Evelina attempted to lend her assistance, something strange happened.

"You're a failure!" a woman's voice echoed. "You'll never succeed!" another voice joined in, distant yet haunting. "You're not worthy!" A man's shout pierced through the chaos. "Please help me!" A voice wept, "I can't handle this anymore..."

Instead of connecting with Nadia alone, she began to hear a cacophony of voices, a chorus of fears from all those who had attempted to pass through the Void Nexus before. Out to Evelina, pleading for her help, their anxieties reverberating through her being. Overwhelmed by the multitude of fears bombarding her consciousness, Evelina struggled to discern her voice from the collective clamor.

Lost amidst the symphony of fears, Evelina faced her greatest fear: the fear of losing herself amid others' anxieties. It was a fear she had never confronted before, and the magnitude of it threatened to consume her. Once solid and steadfast, Evelina felt her confidence waver as she grappled with the tidal wave of fears crashing against her.

During Evelina's struggle, Orville, the hermaphroditic seahorse, was caught in a whirlwind of self-doubt. As he observed his companions fighting their fears, he couldn't help but question his own worth. Comparing his relatively diminutive size to the grandeur of the mermaids, Orville felt a sense of inadequacy creep into his thoughts. Whenever his attention turned outward, focusing on appearances and the outside world, he fell into the trap of comparison.

As Orville ventured deeper into the Void Nexus, the cacophony of conflicting voices surrounded him, amplifying his inner turmoil.

"You're stronger than you think, Orville," his inner warrior said, attempting to lift him. But the cold, mocking tone swiftly responded, "Stop kidding. You have no strength, you little seahorse."

"I'll be alright. I'll be alright," Orville reassured himself, trying to quell the rising doubts. However, the relentless voice of self-doubt persisted, whispering, "Forget about it. You're not going to conquer this void."

Forgetting his nature and true essence, Orville became lost in a cycle of self-judgment. He started to change his gender in a desperate attempt to define himself, believing that he could escape his own fears by becoming someone else. Each transformation brought forth a different persona within him. In one moment, he embodied the image of a strong warrior, convincing himself to face his fears head-on. But in the next moment, he transformed into a coward, consumed by the desire to flee from the challenges that lay before him. Then, he would morph into a wise sage, only to be followed by a panic attack that left him paralyzed with fear.

Amidst the chaos of his ever-shifting mind, Orville found himself circling in place, unable to move forward or backward. His indecision became a prison, trapping him in a cycle of self-doubt and uncertainty. The more he changed his mind, the more lost he became in the labyrinth of his own fears.

The Melody of Rebirth

As Orville spun in his bewildered state, something remarkable occurred. The rock he carried within his brood pouch began to vibrate, sending a surge of energy throughout his being. A thin ocean current, seemingly defying the rules of the Void Nexus, emerged and flowed toward him. Orville's eyes widened in astonishment as he tracked its trajectory, unable to comprehend its origin.

Before he could react, the current struck his brood pouch, causing the rock to respond with a pulsating vibration reminiscent of a heartbeat. A radiant diamond ray shot forth from the rock in that fleeting moment, illuminating the previously dark void. Orville felt cradled within the warm embrace of the diamond ray, and a profound sense of peace and loving energy encircled him.

All his fears seemed to start melting away in that instant as if they were mere illusions. The grip of self-doubt loosened on Orville's mind, and a newfound clarity washed over him. He understood that his worth was not contingent upon his size or appearance but resided within the unique essence of his being.

The loving energy that emanated from the diamond ray infused every fiber of Orville's being, reminding him of his inherent value and purpose. It whispered to him, urging him to relinquish his self-imposed limitations and embrace his true potential.

Empowered by this newfound realization, Orville shed the shackles of comparison and self-judgment. He chose to no longer focus on his external attributes but instead embraced the strength that lay within his heart. With each passing moment, his confidence grew, and he felt a surge of love and acceptance for himself.

Guided by the warm currents of the diamond ray, Orville decided to leave behind his incessant mind games and embrace a new approach. He carried the vibrating rock, no longer seeking to change himself or prove his worth. Instead, he swam toward his fellow merfolk without any agenda.

Now free from the burden of his fears, Orville's presence became a beacon of unyielding support and acceptance. He embodied the calm and loving energy he had experienced, allowing it to radiate from his very being. His companions, caught in their battles with fear, began to sense Orville's genuine presence.

One by one, they felt the transformative power of his calm and loving energy, and the grip of their fears began to loosen. Resistance melted away as they surrendered to the current of calmness and peace that Orville carried with him. The whispers of fear grew fainter, drowned out by the symphony of tranquility resonating within them.

The merfolk found solace in the tranquil flow, feeling like they were cradled within the nurturing embrace of a mother's womb. The journey became less about conquering fear and more about surrendering to the inherent wisdom within themselves. They allowed the current of loving energy to guide them, trusting that it would lead them to their truest selves.

In this collective state of serenity, the merfolk realized the strength that unity brought. Each one carried unique fears and challenges, yet they drew strength from one another's presence. The radiant diamond ray continued to shine, lighting their path and reminding them of the infinite well of love and support they shared.

As time lost its meaning within the depths of the Void Nexus, the merfolk and Orville swam in a blissful state of oneness, their hearts intertwined in a symphony of trust and harmony. Hours or days seemed to pass in an instant as they reveled in the beauty of their connectedness.

Suddenly, a brilliant light beckoned them ahead, casting a warm glow upon the surrounding waters. With eager anticipation, they followed the shimmering path and found themselves at the entrance of a magnificent city. It was a place where the transcendent essence of the water met the grandeur of an unknown civilization.

"We made it!" Nadia's voice echoed through the city, filled with joy and triumph. The merfolk swam and leaped with joy. Their movements synchronized to celebrate their newfound liberation. They allowed the cascading waters of the giant waterfall to drench their bodies, feeling its refreshing spray as a blessing for their rebirth.

Amidst the jubilant revelry, Orville, carrying the rock adorned with the radiant diamond ray, felt a surge of gratitude and awe wash over him. The warm, loving energy that had enveloped him throughout their journey filled his heart. With a sense of profound connection to his fellow merfolk and the mystical power within the rock, he joined in the celebration.

Orville swam gracefully through the vibrant currents, his every movement reflecting the brilliance of the diamond ray. As he circled his companions, his presence emanated a mesmerizing glow, captivating the attention of those around him. The merfolk marveled at the sight, their eyes drawn to the magnificent fusion of light and water surrounding Orville and the rock.

☆

At this point, Evelina's senses tingling with curiosity, gracefully followed the gentle current that had guided them through the depths of the Void Nexus. The enchanting melody carried by the current beckoned her further into the heart of the city. Each note whispered promises of wonder and discovery, fueling her desire to unravel the mysteries that awaited her.

As she swam deeper into the city, the harmonious music grew in intensity, like an irresistible melody whispering its secrets to her soul, pulling her closer with an undeniable allure. The vibrant sounds wove through the ethereal pathways, meandering through a realm where time and space seemed to meld together. They harmonized with the ocean breeze, creating an enchanting symphony saturated the surroundings with a mystical ambiance. The current, now tinged with the hues of anticipation, guided her to the heart of the majestic waterfall.

As Evelina approached, a breathtaking sight greeted her eyes. Layers of rainbows, vibrant and alive, arched gracefully above the cascading waters. They created a shimmering tapestry of colors that seemed to defy the boundaries of imagination.

Evelina couldn't resist the allure of the mesmerizing rainbows. With each stroke of her tail, she drew nearer to the heart of the waterfall, feeling the misty droplets caress her skin like delicate kisses from the ocean itself. The radiant colors danced in harmony, casting a spell of awe and wonder upon all who beheld them.

As she swam closer, Evelina was surrounded by a divine symphony of light and sound. The rainbow hues shimmered with a mesmerizing luminescence, painting the waters and the city with breathtaking magical brilliance. The enchanting music, now resonating with newfound clarity, seemed to emanate from the very heart of the rainbows.

Evelina was surrounded by a divine symphony of light and sound as she swam closer. The rainbow hues shimmered with a mesmerizing luminescence, painting the waters and the city with breathtaking magical brilliance. The enchanting music resonated with newfound clarity, emanating from the very heart of the rainbows.

Lost in the magical embrace of the rainbows, Evelina swam deeper into the heart of the waterfall. The current, now intertwined with the enchanting melody, guided her with a gentle yet purposeful force. It led her through a shimmering portal, where she found herself in a realm bathed in transcendental radiance and pulsating with boundless energy.

Evelina felt the whispers of ancient wisdom caress her spirit in this realm of infinite possibilities. The air hummed with the echoes of forgotten tales and untold journeys. Evelina immersed herself in the current of melody emanating from the vibrant rainbow. With every passing moment, she allowed herself to be carried deeper into its rhythm, surrendering to its enchanting embrace.

As the melodies caressed her senses, a profound realization swept over her like a gentle wave washing over the shore. It became clear to her that this was more than just a beautiful song; it was a beckoning call, a resounding invitation to awaken the dormant magic within everyone.

With each note that resonated through her being, Evelina felt the stirring of ancient energies, awakening long-forgotten powers that had slumbered within her soul. The melodies reached into the depths of her being, coaxing the magic to rise to the surface. It was like the rainbow had become a conduit, a bridge connecting her to grand mysteries.

While Evelina was fully immersed in the transformative melody, she suddenly sensed the awe emanating from her fellow merfolk. Intrigued and curious, she swiftly swam back to join them, eager to share her discoveries. However, what she witnessed left her speechless.

The majestic marine creatures she had never seen surrounded the bright diamond beam radiating from Orville's brood pouch. Their elegant figures swirled and spun in a captivating dance, their presence emanating profound wisdom and ancient power. They joined their voices in harmony, echoing what Evelina had heard from the rainbow waterfall.

"What are they?" Evelina marveled, her voice tinged with awe and excitement.

"Definitely not dragons," Triton said, gazing at the exquisite beings' captivating dance. Their incredible cadence moved his heart, and he couldn't take his eye away from it.

The merfolk stood in awe, their eyes wide with wonder. It was a sight beyond their wildest dreams, a convergence of magic and harmony that filled their hearts with a renewed sense of purpose. As the melodic symphony resonated through the city and beyond, the merfolk felt the vibration of each note reverberate within their souls, awakening their own latent magic.

As Evelina drew nearer, she couldn't help but marvel at the sight before her. Once nestled within Orville's brood pouch, the rock gradually floated into the open waters. It radiated a mesmerizing brilliance, rivaling even the most exquisite diamonds. Every facet of the stone glimmered with an ethereal glow, casting a delicate, shimmering light that danced harmoniously alongside the enchanting majestic marine creatures surrounding it.

The light emitted by the rock intertwines with the singing of the giant creatures, creating a bewitching symphony of illumination and sound. Each movement and note was a testament to their shared unity and synchronicity. It was like the very essence of the melody had manifested itself in the radiance of the rock, amplifying its majestic power.

The vibrant hues of the rock echoed the enchanting sounds of the giant creatures as though they were engaged in a secret conversation, exchanging secrets known only to them. The gentle hum of the creatures' songs resonated through the water, blending seamlessly with the shimmering light. It was a harmonious display, a divine collaboration between the living beings and the radiant rock.

The intimate bond between the enormous beings and the rock captured Evelina's attention. Their movements appeared to be orchestrated in perfect synchrony, mirroring the pulsating rhythm of the light. They responded to the rock's dazzling hints with grace and elegance as if they knew its language. Evelina was in awe of this captivating underwater display as the symphony of their interplay produced a surreal atmosphere where the lines between sound and light dissolved.

As Evelina immersed herself in the intriguing interplay between the rock and the enigmatic creatures, she couldn't shake the feeling that the stone possessed extraordinary power. This power guided the creatures, commanding their responses with an almost mystical influence. The enigma surrounding the rock only fueled Evelina's curiosity, leaving her more intrigued.

Evelina turned to Orville with bated breath, hoping he had solved the riddles hidden within the rock. She couldn't stop asking, "Orville, have you unlocked the secrets of the rock?"

Orville's smile held a sense of mystery and wisdom as he continued, "It seems the riddle only guides us here, but it may not hold all the answers."

Intrigued by Orville's response, Triton interjected, "Aren't riddles supposed to have all the answers to lead us directly to the truth?"

"Not always, my friend," Orville said after pausing to consider Triton's question. "Sometimes the true significance of the riddle lies not in the answers it provides but in the journey it sets in motion. The outcome, the final revelation, is yet to be formed and presented. We need to be patient and have faith in the process."

Curiosity flickered in Nadia's eyes as she asked, "What does that mean, Orville? How can we make our way through this journey if the answers are elusive?"

With a calm and reassuring tone, Orville replied, "The enigmatic nature of the rock's mysteries invites us to embark on a path of exploration and self-discovery. The true essence of the rock lies not in quick answers but in its transformative power. Through this journey, we will gain insights, gather wisdom, and ultimately uncover the truth. We must embrace the unknown because the journey to discover its secrets has just begun."

Evelina, resonating with Orville's words, felt a renewed sense of purpose. She watched in awe as the marine creatures swam gracefully around the diamond ray, their movements synchronized and fluid. They channeled their collective energy, infusing it with the enchanting melody reverberating through the depths. Their presence exuded a profound sense of ancient wisdom feeling like they were guardians of the magical realm they inhabited.

In this enchanting spectacle, Evelina felt a surge of inspiration and connection. It seemed the giant creatures were inviting her to join their dance, to add her voice to their harmonies. With reverence, she positioned herself amidst the swirling currents and began to sing.

Her voice blended seamlessly with the melody, resonating with the luminous energy that enveloped them all. Together, they created a symphony that transcended the boundaries of the underwater realm, reaching into the very depths of the merfolk's souls.

As the melody echoed through the underwater city, Nadia and Triton, who had once been held captive by their fears, now felt a newfound sense of liberation. They joined Evelina and the marine creatures in their mesmerizing dance, their voices intertwining in harmonious layers that added depth and richness to the ever-evolving symphony.

Surrounded by the ethereal presence of the singing merfolk, the marine creatures, and the radiant diamond ray, the water around them pulsated with harmonious energy. Waves of shimmering golden light cascaded through the depths, creating a luminous aura extending far beyond the underwater city's boundaries. The enchanting symphony they wove together resonated within their own realm and transcended dimensions, capturing the attention of beings from the Earth and celestial planes alike.

The mesmerizing melodies of the merpeople and marine creatures reverberated through the fathomless depths of the underwater realm. Their ethereal tunes were intricately woven with the magic of Queen Meridia's crafting shield.

A wondrous transformation unfolded as the melodic currents intertwined with the shimmering energy shield. The shield seemed to come alive, pulsating with a radiant light that danced harmoniously with the celestial melodies. Suddenly, the shield acted as a gateway, allowing their songs to transcend the confines of the underwater realm and resonate with unparalleled clarity and potency, echoing all the way to the mermaid kingdom.

Within the grand coral palace, Queen Meridia stood by the shimmering energy shield that surrounded her. She attuned to the vibrations of the energy shield. She sensed the successful passage of her merfolk through the void of whispering. She closed her eyes and allowed the residual vibrations of the enchanting melody to wash over her.

"They made it," Queen Meridia's heart was filled with immense pride and joy as she spoke to her trusted advisor, Zephyr, who stood by her side. She could feel the thrill rising as her dream of restoring the world's vibrancy and ocean magic drew closer.

Zephyr's eyes sparkled with admiration for his queen and the merfolk who had ventured into the void of whispering. "Indeed, Your Majesty," he replied, his voice tinged with reverence. "They have proven their courage and unity, and their success is a testament to the strength of their spirits and the bond they share."

The strong wave of magical unification connected the underwater city with the celestial beings. It was a bridge for the mermaid kingdom to experience something beyond their familiar water life. The melodies transmitted through the energy shield brought the mermaid kingdom into harmony with the celestial realms, granting them a glimpse into the boundless wonders of the universe.

The tunes swept over the mermaid realm, enveloping the people in delight. The waves appeared to reflect the heavenly tapestry above as they shimmered with dazzling tints. The underwater life performed graceful dances. Their actions were in time with the transcendent music. Every mermaid and merman experienced a burst of inspiration and a profound connection to the energies of the cosmos.

Along the intriguing vibrations of singing and the radiant light, a wondrous phenomenon began to unfold — an opening of a diamond ray light portal extending from the depths of the underwater city to the surface. Its existence seemed woven with magic and mystery, revealing a gateway to unseen realms.

As the harmonies swelled, the vibrations grew stronger, causing ripples to cascade through the water. The merfolk felt the power of their united voices resonating through their bodies, igniting a profound sense of connection with the water elements and the celestial forces that watched over them. Evelina, immersed in the euphoria of the moment, could sense the presence of otherworldly beings drawn to the extraordinary display of magic and harmony.

Guided by the diamond ray consciousness, the waves became sentient, flowing with purpose and intention. They surged towards the vast expanse of the ocean, where the moonlight gracefully danced upon the water's surface. The diamond ray merged seamlessly with the moon's ethereal glow, their combined radiance illuminating the darkness of the night.

The ocean shimmered as if studded with countless diamonds, their collective brilliance transforming the seascape into a spectacle of luminescence. Waves glistened with an otherworldly light, creating a breathtaking vista that defied imagination. It looked like a colossal, celestial diamond had taken form, casting its radiant glow across the vast expanse of the ocean, illuminating even the deepest corners of the night.

The miracle continued to unfold, and as the diamond ray merged with the moonlight, the night sky responded in kind. Stars twinkled with newfound brilliance, casting their shimmering light onto the ocean's surface, creating a celestial mirror that reflected the grandeur of the heavens.

Orville and Merfolk's eyes widened with awe as she beheld this magnificent sight. The merging of the diamond ray and moonlight was a harmonious union. This celestial collaboration filled their hearts with wonder and reverence. They could feel the presence of ancient beings, drawn to the extraordinary display of magic and harmony unfolding before them. They understood they had witnessed a rare convergence of elemental forces and mystical energies at that moment.

.Twelve.
Sunset Sailing

12

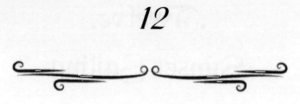

As the gang gathered at the hidden nature harbor, known only to Hank, an air of excitement and anticipation encircled them. The sun gracefully descended, casting a radiant golden glow across the sky. The clouds transformed into a picturesque canvas, where hues of orange and pink intertwined, creating a mesmerizing display of nature's artistry.

It felt like the universe had conspired to set the stage for an extraordinary evening filled with adventure and the promise of new discoveries. The gang couldn't help but be captivated by the enchanting scene, feeling a sense of awe and gratitude for being a part of this magical moment.

"Guys, let's go," Hank called out, his voice filled with a renewed sense of purpose. The gang turned to look at him, their eyes widening in surprise and delight. Hank's appearance was a testament to his inner transformation, a reflection of the trust and belief the young gang had instilled in him. With a contagious smile, he approached his friends, who greeted him with cheers and infectious smiles.

As Hank stepped out of his boat, a sense of awe washed over the gang. Once tousled and unkempt, his hair was now neatly styled, catching the glimmers of the setting sun and reflecting his inner radiance. Dressed in casual yet effortlessly stylish attire, Hank exuded an air of confidence and adventure.

The gang couldn't help but be captivated by Hank's transformation. It seemed a dormant fire had been reignited within him, infusing his presence with a magnetic aura. They exchanged glances, their eyes reflecting a mix of surprise, admiration, and anticipation for the adventure that awaited them.

Hank approached his friends with a beaming smile, their cheers and applause filling the air. The harbor buzzed with excitement as everyone gathered around, eager to glimpse Hank's newfound confidence and share in the joy of his transformation. The gang couldn't contain their enthusiasm, each member cheering and offering encouragement.

"I can't believe my dreams since a child is now becoming a reality," Lily exclaimed, her voice resonating with a sense of awe and the magical orchestration of the universe.

She boarded Hank's boat with graceful steps, representing the gateway to their adventure. The rest of the gang joined her, their hearts brimming with excitement and a shared sense of anticipation for the enchanting journey that awaited them.

Like strokes from a celestial artist's brush, the clouds painted a majestic tableau in the sky. The atmosphere was charged with palpable energy, the air filled with infinite possibilities and the anticipation of a truly extraordinary evening ahead.

As twilight descended, a breathtaking sight unfolded above them. Unlike its usual appearance, the moon began to rise while the sky retained remnants of daylight. Its radiant glow painted the heavens with a celestial brushstroke, casting an ethereal light upon the tranquil waters below. The gang stood in awe, captivated by the uncommon spectacle that filled their hearts with wonder.

"The moon is out early today," Giselle exclaimed, her voice tinged with excitement.

"It's the first supermoon of this year. We are in for a truly magical evening," Sara added, her eyes glistening with excitement.

"Why? Jewell is going to transform?" Wild jokingly interjected, prompting laughter from the group.

Their lighthearted banter filled the air, dissolving any remnants of lingering tension or worries.

Under the night sky, Hank steered the boat with expertise and a contagious sense of adventure. The gentle sway of the waves and the cool breeze caressing their faces heightened their sense of freedom and exhilaration. They sailed along the shimmering waters, their laughter and joy echoing in harmony with the rhythm of the ocean.

As they sailed, the moon's luminous glow seemed to infuse the surroundings with a touch of enchantment. The water sparkled like a sea of diamonds, mirroring the celestial beauty above. The air was alive with the whispers of nature, carrying with it a sense of mystery and untold stories.

Their journey carried them past hidden coves and secret isles, each offering a glimpse into a world untouched by time. The sound of distant melodies filled the air as if the very essence of the night had taken the form of ethereal music.

As the moon ascended higher in the sky, its radiance intensified, casting a silvery glow over everything it touched. It seemed to awaken the dormant magic within the hearts of the gang, igniting their imaginations and filling them with a sense of wonder.

Amidst the laughter and joy, Fergus couldn't help but wonder about Wild's earlier discovery. An air of mystery surrounded it, like a secret waiting to be unveiled. However, he trusted Wild's intuition and let the moment pass for now, embracing the magic of the evening and the bond they shared.

The group was in awe of faraway constellations dotting the sky as the boat continued cruising through the night, their brilliance contributing to the atmosphere. Their faces were stroked by a soft breeze that carried an air of calm expectation. Hank seemed to be lost in contemplation as he steadily piloted the boat.

"Hank, where are we heading to?" G.T. broke the silence, curiosity lacing his voice.

All eyes turned to Hank, expecting a confident response. However, to their surprise, he wore a strange look on his face and hesitated before replying. "To be honest, I'm not quite sure," he admitted, his voice tinged with vulnerability and determination.

The gang was taken aback, their gazes fixed on Hank, waiting for an explanation.

A moment of uncertainty and strange silence settled among the gang, the weight of Hank's words hanging in the air. G.T.'s brow furrowed with confusion as he asked again, "What do you mean?"

Hank laughed, embarrassed, feeling the weight of their expectations pressing upon him. "I've spent years trying to recreate the exact path I took to meet the unicorn, hoping to unlock its magic once more, but... I've come up empty-handed," he admitted, his voice trailing.

Silent glances were exchanged among the gang, their expressions a mix of surprise and disappointment. The idea of embarking on this adventure had ignited a spark of hope within them, a hope that they would rediscover the extraordinary encounter Hank had once experienced. Now, confronted with the reality that it might not be possible, a sense of uncertainty settled within their hearts.

A deep contemplative silence fell upon the group as they grappled with their thoughts and doubts. The realization that Hank's fruitless pursuit washed over them, leaving a sense of unease and uncertainty in its wake.

Giselle, known for her unwavering determination, broke the silence, her eyes narrowing with curiosity. "Why did you rush back to the cottage this morning?" she inquired, her voice laced with intrigue.

G.T. joined in, adding his voice to the growing curiosity. "And the wooden necklace... You took it straight away," he remarked, his tone echoing the collective intrigue of the gang.

Hank took a deep breath, the weight of his confession heavy upon him. "I was searching for answers, for a way to repeat that magical encounter," he began. "This morning, it suddenly hit me that there was one thing I had overlooked all these years. I had tried to replicate every factor, down to the smallest details like the music and clothes I wore, but I never gave the necklace any thought."

Hank's voice carried a tinge of regret as he continued, "The necklace is an heirloom that has been passed down through generations in my family. It has significant personal value. I wore it on that fateful day when I came across the unicorns. Yet, I took it off the day after and left it in the cottage."

The gang listened intently, their curiosity piqued by the revelation.

Sara's eyes shimmered with wonder as she examined the necklace more closely. "It must hold a special power," she mused, her voice filled with awe.

Hank nodded, a mix of nostalgia and anticipation in his eyes. "That's what I've come to believe," he replied. "The necklace represents a connection to the magic I seek, a missing link I hadn't realized until now."

Hank took a moment to gather his thoughts, the weight of his realization settling upon him. "You see, as a professor engaged in marine research, I've always followed the scientific approaches, searching for logical explanations for the phenomena I've encountered. Magic was never a factor I considered. However, now I understand that what I experienced that night goes beyond scientific explanation," he confessed, his voice tinged with awe and vulnerability.

G.T.'s eyes widened with newfound understanding. "So, you think the necklace played a role in your encounter with the unicorn?" he asked, his voice filled with anticipation.

Hank nodded, his gaze meeting each member of the gang. "I can't be certain, but it's the only variable I haven't been able to replicate.

As Hank spoke, realization dawned on the gang. With its deep-rooted history and connection to Hank's past, the necklace held a significance he hadn't considered before. It was a missing piece of the puzzle, a link to the magic they were searching for.

A sense of possibility filled the air, and the gang exchanged glances, their minds buzzing with the potential implications of the necklace. It held the promise of unlocking the secrets of their journey, of reconnecting with the enchantment Hank had once experienced.

"Well, let's pray for a miracle tonight," Hank added, trying to cheer up the group with a glint of hope in his eyes.

The air was charged with a mix of anticipation and determination. "Certainly, fortune always favors the bold!" Giselle chimed in, her voice brimming with unwavering confidence.

Sara, unable to contain her mischievous spirit, flashed Jewell a playful wink. "Looks like we're going to awaken black jaguar tonight," she teased, her words filled with anticipation and excitement.

"I didn't know we had a spirit junkie here," Hank said with a smile, his eyes sparkling with understanding. Sara's playful comment had struck a chord within him, and he sensed the deeper meaning behind her words. The gang chuckled at Hank's lighthearted response, feeling a sense of unity and camaraderie.

Amidst the laughter, Wild's voice broke through the excitement and uncertainty. "Is Jewell really going to transform tonight?" he asked, his tone a mixture of excitement and trepidation.

All eyes turned to Jewell, whose gaze held a mix of anticipation and a touch of suspicion.

Jewell's expression turned playful as she considered Wild's question. "Okay, how about we awaken the black jaguar now?" She proclaimed, a mischievous gleam in her eyes. "However, before we proceed, let me ask you all. What comes to you when you think about black jaguars?"

The gang pondered for a moment, each member sharing their thoughts individually. "Fear," one said. "Danger," another chimed in. "Speed," "Strength," "Unknown," "transformation," the responses flowed like a river. Jewell listened intently, nodding at each answer.

Jewell said with a smile flickering on her lips, "Well, whatever associations you have with black jaguars, it represents what echoes with you right now. It portrays the strengths and inner challenges waiting to be discovered and overcome in each of us."

Wild, ever the joker, couldn't resist chiming in. "So, we need to be patient, venture into the unknown, conquer our fears, and maybe even undergo a transformation tonight?" he quipped, his voice a playful blend of humor and wisdom.

Jewell's smile widened, her eyes sparkling with agreement. "Exactly!" she exclaimed. "We set out on this journey not only to awaken the spirit of the black jaguar but also to discover our own hidden strengths and navigate the challenges that lie ahead. It's a journey of self-discovery and transformation.

Shamans saw the black jaguar as a powerful spirit guide, capable of accompanying and protecting them as they spanned between the physical and supernatural realms. They believed the black jaguar symbolized the ability to move through the darkness and navigate the unknown with grace and confidence. In this journey, we too can tap into the wisdom and guidance of the black jaguar to help us transform and embrace our true potential."

The gang exchanged knowing glances, excitement, and resolution evident in their eyes. They were ready to embrace the journey, to face the unknown with courage and resilience. The spirit of the black jaguar had awakened something within them, an unwavering belief in their potential.

As they set sail under the luminous moonlight, a sense of unity and purpose enveloped the gang. They were connected by a shared mission, drawn together by fate and the magic of their intertwined stories. The black jaguar's spirit beckoned them onward. With each passing moment, they felt their spirits grow bolder, stronger, and more attuned to the mysteries that awaited them.

As the boat sailed into the night, the gang couldn't help but revel in the magical atmosphere surrounding them. The moonlight cast an ethereal glow upon the water while the gentle breeze whispered ancient secrets through the air.

Wild's Encounter

"Guys, I found unicorns!" Wild shouted, his voice brimming with excitement. Everyone ran to where Wild was pointing at a school of fish on the boat's port side.

Giselle gave Wild's shoulder a playful tap. "Don't tease us. They're simply fish," she said with a smile.

To everyone's surprise, however, the fish had a unique feature.

"Pay attention. They, have horns, too," said Wild.

Hank, wearing a knowing smile, identified the

fish with a hint of amusement in his voice. "Those are blue spine unicorn fish," he explained, gesturing toward their distinctively bony horn.

The gang laughed, amused by the unexpected encounter with underwater unicorns.

"I prefer to see mermaids," G.T. complained playfully.

Wild rolled up his left sleeve without missing a beat, revealing a beautifully colored mermaid tattoo. "Mermaid? Here you go," he said with a naughty grin.

G.T. couldn't help but examine the tattoo closely, surprised by Wild's fondness for mermaids. "I didn't know you're a fan of mermaids," G.T. asked, his voice tinted with curiosity.

Giselle jokingly leaned on Wild and said, "He almost got married to a mermaid!"

Wild chuckled and nodded in agreement. "She's right."

Fergus, who had been quiet up until this point, now speaks. He asked, his eyes wide with curiosity, "Say again?"

"None of you would believe it, but this young gentleman in front of you was once the youngest free diving champion in the world," Giselle revealed, her voice filled with admiration.

Wild nodded and bowed funny to everyone,

acknowledging Giselle's revelation. A smile of pride played on his lips as he basked in the group's admiration.

G.T. couldn't believe what he had just heard, his eyes widening with surprise. The rest of the gang looked at Wild with a newfound sense of marvel and admiration, their curiosity piqued, eager to learn more about his remarkable feat.

"I bet you were chasing after pretty mermaids, and that's how you got the champion," Sara playfully teased, a mischievous twinkle in her eyes.

Lily joined in the excitement, her curiosity piqued. "Tell us more about your diving adventures!" she urged, her voice filled with anticipation.

The gang leaned in closer, eager to hear the captivating tales of Wild's underwater explorations and the enchanting encounters he had experienced beneath the waves.

Wild chuckled at Sara's playful remark, his eyes twinkling with a hint of nostalgia. "Well, it's not far from the truth," he admitted with a grin. "Growing up, I was always fascinated by the stories of mermaids, and it was my love for the ocean that led me on this incredible journey."

Wild halted, pausing to collect his thoughts. He began, "Well, where to begin..." His eyes glistened in anticipation of telling a story profoundly ingrained in his childhood. "A mermaid legend was fashioned into all of our lives in the place where I grew up."

His voice was tinged with reverence as he leaned forward. "Mermaids were revered as the guardians and protectors of the ocean and an integral part of Mother Earth's spirit. Given that the oceans occupy more than 70% of our planet's surface, it should come as no surprise. They had a special connection to the elements of water and marine life. They guarded those who deeply bonded with the ocean's mysteries."

A hushed silence fell upon the group as they absorbed the profoundness of the mermaid legend. Lily's eyes sparkled with wonder, her imagination painting vivid pictures of majestic beings concealed within the ocean's depths.

With a gleam in his eye, Wild said, "But that's not all. The extraordinary power that mermaids possessed was invisible to human eyes. They could alter themselves into a golden, glistening light near people, protecting them from harm."

Lily's breath caught, her mind swirling with enchanting images of mermaids graced with ethereal radiance. "That's stunning," she breathed, her voice mixed with amazement and fascination.

Wild nodded, his lips moving in a gentle smile.

"It is, in fact, my strong desire to discover the ocean's secrets and come face to face with the hidden treasures beneath the waves was sparked by the legends of these mysterious beings when I was a young child."

As the group listened intently, Wild's voice gained impetus. "It was during my childhood explorations that I had my most extraordinary encounter. I had dived into the ocean's depths, enveloped by a world teeming with life and vibrant hues. And there, in a moment that transcended ordinary existence, I witnessed the manifestation of the mermaid's presence."

The group leaned forward, hanging onto Wild's every word, their imaginations ignited by the appeal of an extraordinary adventure.

Wild recounted the incident, his voice bursting with pure awe of it. "A golden light, like a divine aura, encircled me, casting a magical glow that touched every corner of the underwater realm," Wild said. "The mermaid's essence seemed to have entwined with my soul, and I felt a deep connection and an unspoken understanding."

The group gasped, their minds filled with the magnificence of the scene Wild described. The moment's weight settled upon them, carrying a shared appreciation for the mermaid's hidden presence and the depth of the ocean's secrets.

"With that encounter, my diving journey took on a new purpose," Wild continued, his tone filled with determination. "I realized my passion for exploring the depths was not merely about breaking records or conquering challenges. It was about connecting with the ocean's spirit, honoring the guardians who watched over it, and sharing its beauty with the world."

Lily's eyes shone with a newfound understanding, her heart brimming with admiration for Wild's profound reverence for the mermaid and the ocean. A tapestry of enchanting imagery unfolded in her mind—a testament to the power of legends and the infinite wonders that await those who dare to venture beneath the surface.

Moved by the mermaid's tale and the ocean's depths, Lily couldn't contain her emotions. A melody danced upon her lips, and her voice resonated with a tender yet powerful beauty. The words she sang were an ode to the mermaids, a heartfelt tribute to their mystery and grace.

As the first notes escaped her lips, the rest of the group fell into a serene silence, captivated by the purity and warmth of Lily's voice. Her song seemed to carry the essence of the ocean itself, swirling with currents of longing and reverence.

Her voice soared, echoing through the air like it reached out to the very depths of the sea. Each word painted vivid images of mermaids gliding through turquoise waters, their colorful tails shimmering under the sun's gentle caress. It was a song that celebrated the human spirit's interconnectedness and the mermaids' enchanting realm.

As the last note faded into the ether, an ethereal silence hung in the air. The group remained still, absorbing the lingering magic that the song had left behind. They exchanged glances, their eyes shining with a newfound appreciation for Lily's talent and the mermaid's mystique.

Wild's voice trembled as he spoke, his appreciation brimming over. "Lily, wow! Your music... really made me feel something. It seems you give the mermaids new life, and they are now here with us, guiding us on this amazing voyage."

The group nodded in agreement, their smiles beaming with gratitude for Lily's heartfelt contribution. They had an unbreakable bond, feeling like the mermaids' hearts had merged with their own, propelling them to embark on a remarkable journey.

Lily blushed, her eyes glistening with happiness and modesty. "I'm just thrilled my song could capture the magic we all feel inside."

Hank stated with an honest and earnest tone, "Lily, there's something I need to share with you." He met Lily's eyes, laced with shyness and anticipation. "The melody you sang in front of the Rainbow Waterfall... It's the same tunes I heard when encountering the unicorns."

Lily's eyes widened in disbelief as Hank's words hung in the air. The rest of the gang stared at him, their jaws dropping in astonishment.

G.T. couldn't contain his disbelief and blurted out, "That's the craziest thing I've ever heard!"

Hank nodded, his expression earnest. "I know it sounds unbelievable, but it's true," he insisted.

"As I enthralled myself in the sea's breathtaking depths, a magical scene unfolded. A radiant herd of unicorns surrounded me while a portal of shimmering galaxies materialized in the watery expanse. And in that moment, the same enchanting melody you sang filled the air, echoing through the depths. I couldn't believe my ears when I heard it this morning."

The gang sat in stunned silence, their minds struggling to process the sheer magnitude of Hank's revelation. The serendipity of Lily's song intertwining with Hank's encounter with the unicorns felt like a convergence of fantastical tales.

Lily leaned forward, her eyes sparkling with curiosity. "That's why you asked about the melody this morning," she clamored, her voice brimming with excitement.

"Hank, please, tell us more about the unicorns! What were they like? Did they possess magical powers?" Her eagerness was infectious, and the room buzzed with a renewed sense of anticipation.

Hank smiled, his voice tinged with nostalgia. "The unicorns... they were truly magnificent. Their coats glistened like moonlit dew, and their eyes shimmered with ancient wisdom. There was an undeniable aura of magic that surrounded them. They possessed an innate ability to bring solace and restoration, physically and spiritually," he continued.

"In their presence, I felt a profound sense of tranquility and serenity, as though the unicorns carried the essence of purity and hope within them."

The group listened closely, their minds racing with images of unicorns riding through wondrous galaxies and bringing magic to all they encountered.

With a heartfelt sincerity, Hank began to share his story, the weight of his emotions palpable in the air.

"To be honest," he said softly, "I met the unicorns on the day of my grandmother's funeral. She was the last family I had left after losing my parents in an accident." A moment of reflection settled upon him as he gathered the courage to continue. "After the funeral, I found she had left me a wooden necklace and a letter."

Hank paused, his emotions tugging at his heart. "I must admit, I had been rebellious towards my grandma since my parent's death. I carried a burden of regrets and unresolved feelings. So, in the depths of my grief when she passed away, I made a decision. I boarded my boat and set sail, desperate to escape, to find solace as far away as possible."

The gang listened attentively, their faces reflecting a mix of sympathy and understanding. They realized the depth of Hank's pain and the significance of his encounter with the unicorns on such a pivotal day.

Lily's eyes glistened with compassion as she gently asked, "And then, you met the unicorns later that night?"

Hank nodded, gratitude evident in his gaze. "Yes," he confirmed, his voice carrying a hint of awe. "It was in the quiet darkness of the night that the unicorns appeared to me. Their presence, their serene grace, seemed to surround me with soothing energy. I felt a profound connection to something greater than myself at that moment. It was as if the unicorns, with their gentle presence, were offering me comfort and understanding."

The gang exchanged glances, touched by the significance of Hank's encounter. They recognized that the unicorns had become a symbol of hope and healing, providing Hank with solace during a time of immense grief and guilt.

Hank continued, his voice steady but filled with emotion. "In their company, I found solace and forgiveness within myself. The unicorns reminded me of the unconditional love and strength my grandmother had shown me throughout my life. They carried a message of acceptance and urged me to embrace the memories of my parents with love and gratitude rather than regrets. That's also the first time in my life I felt I was connected to greater power and belonging."

"That's why you're hunting them like crazy, even sacrificing your promising career?" Fergus asked, his voice tinged with curiosity and concern.

Hank sighed, a touch of regret and thoughtfulness appearing in his gaze. "What an irony," he mused.

"I gave in to the allure of that enchanted night and allowed myself to be taken away by it, despite all the caring voices and cautions from everyone around me. An unknown force seemed to call me and whispered softly in my ear. I couldn't tell then if I chose this road to avoid facing my grief or because something bigger was calling to me."

He stopped, staring off into the distance as his mind wandered into the recesses of his memories. "I lost sight of the costs and sacrifices it took as I was absorbed by the chase. I lost touch with my relationships, stability, and personal well-being. Yet, it was a challenge to realize that when my heart craved something more profound, my outward accomplishments held little meaning."

The group listened intently, their eyes beaming with comprehension. They understood the immense struggle Hank had gone through in trying to strike a balance between his desire for an achieving life in the physical world and the temptation of a world rich in greater connections.

Hank's voice grew softer, his words heavy with reflection. "Despite seeming to lose everything I had from an outside perspective, my heart remained full of something far greater than I could express," he confessed.

"In pursuing the unicorns, I found a deeper connection to the essence of life itself. It was a calling that transcended personal gain, leading me to a realm where the boundaries of ordinary existence blurred and possibilities multiplied. I realized that I was driven not only by the desire for solace or escape but also by an insatiable thirst for meaning and a connection to something greater."

The gang exchanged glances, a mixture of compassion and admiration in their eyes. They understood that Hank's journey had explored his inner depths, driven by a longing for purpose and a yearning to touch the mystical fabric of existence.

Fergus stepped forward, his voice filled with empathy and motivation.

"Hank, thank you for sharing your story. It reminds us that by following our enthusiasm, even if they lead us into uncharted territories, we might eventually discover the true essence of our being."

Hank nodded in agreement, his eyes alight with a newfound sense of purpose.

"You're right, Fergus," he affirmed. "The encounters we have had today, once again, serve as a reminder that the magic of life does exist, regardless of whether we find unicorns tonight or not. These moments of connection and shared experiences are blessings that have enriched my path throughout these years of searching."

The gang, their faces reflecting a mix of admiration and understanding, nodded in agreement.

The Dream of Calling

"I can't believe that a dream could take us this far," Giselle remarked as she grabbed Lily's shoulder and gave her a knowing glance.

Lily nodded, her eyes sparkling with disbelief and wonder. "You're right, Giselle. This journey, this encounter, it's beyond anything I could have imagined," she responded, her voice filled with gratitude.

"It has been a magical day," Sara added a sense of enchantment in her voice.

The gang nodded in agreement, feeling a shared understanding of awe and fulfillment. The weight of their extraordinary experiences lingered in the air, mingling with the whispers of the night.

One by one, they found their place on the deck, lying down and gazing up at the vast expanse of the sky. The stars shimmered above them, painting the canvas of the night with their celestial beauty. The full moon cast a gentle glow, infusing the moment with an ethereal radiance.

As they settled into their spots, a peaceful silence enfolded them. The echoes of their journey resonated within, mingling with the rhythmic lapping of the waves against the hull of the boat. Each one carried a deep appreciation for the remarkable path they had embarked upon and the profound connections they had formed along the way.

Hank, intrigued by their exchange, couldn't help but interject. "So, what exactly was that dream about?" he asked, curiosity evident. He leaned in closer, eager to hear their story and uncover the threads that had led them to this extraordinary moment.

"Since I was a child, I've always had a recurring dream," Lily began, her voice filled with memories. "In this dream, I immersed myself in enchantment and wonder, especially during the full moon. Golden unicorns would radiate an illuminating, shimmering light, their presence captivating my every sense."

Her words hung in the air like admiringly significant childhood dreams that had guided her feet. The group listened closely, their gaze locked on Lily, fascinated by the mysterious nature of her experience.

Lily went on, her voice tinged with wonderment and passion.

"One dream stuck out from the others. It was as

if the waves were whispering ancient secrets, carrying a melody I sang today in front of the waterfall. A tender voice echoed in my dream, resonating with otherworldly wisdom," she explained. "It called out my name, 'Lily,' and revealed that I had a special purpose."

The deck seemed to hold its breath as she spoke, hanging onto every word. The gang leaned in closer, their hearts entwined with Lily's journey.

"It told me to seek a stone hidden beneath the sea," Lily continued, her voice filled with anticipation. "This stone held the key to awakening Princess Acacia and restoring the forgotten magic that had faded from our world."

The revelation was met with a collective gasp from the gang, their eyes wide with astonishment. The pieces of the puzzle were slowly coming together, and the significance of their journey began to unfold.

"Lily, are we living in your dream right now?" Sara questioned as she kept her eyes on the brilliant supermoon above them.

With amazement, G.T. added, "It's strange, yet I can't help but feel the same way."

With a twinkle of understanding in his eyes, Wild nodded in agreement. He continued, "The more I think about it, the more it all falls into place."

The gang paused, a collective realization washing over them. The synchronicities between Lily's dream and their present experience were too apparent to ignore. The full moon, the haunting melody, the whispers of the waves, and the significance of the hidden rock played a part in their extraordinary day.

"You're right, Wild," Lily said, her voice filled with amazement. "Every element of my dream, we almost have encountered it today. It's as if the boundaries between dream and reality have blurred, intertwining our journey with the mystical realm that once seemed only within my imagination."

Jewell joined in, her voice brimming with excitement. "And now, the only missing piece is Princess Acacia herself," she exclaimed, her words filled with anticipation and hope.

"Guys, have you noticed something peculiar about tonight's moon?" Fergus interrupted, his tone filled with intrigue. "It appears different from any moon I've seen before."

Sara chimed in, her voice joining the conversation. "You're right, Fergus. It's the largest supermoon in over a century, or so I've heard. The moon seems to shine with an intensity that captivates the entire sky."

Being the joker, Wild couldn't help but make a witty remark. "Well, I'm still waiting for Jewell's shapeshifting under this extraordinary moonlight," he taunted, drawing amusement from the group.

Fergus continued to offer insights among their laughter, his voice becoming increasingly serious. "However, something extraordinary has caught my attention. It's like a moon-illuminating tree, emitting a delicate radiance that ebbs and flows. And if you look closely, I swear I've noticed glimpses of a diamond-like ray embedded within it. It's very captivating."

The gang fell silent, their focus fixated on Fergus' description. He illustrated an almost surreal sight, a mystical occurrence that eluded understanding.

"And there's more," Fergus said, his voice packed with wonder. "Despite the full moon's illumination tonight, the sky is still filled with countless bright stars. It seems the skies are putting on a spectacle for us, unveiling secrets usually hidden by the moon's radiance."

Lily's eyes widened with surprise and delight as she looked up into the night sky. "This is truly extraordinary," she declared, her voice full of awe.

"The glowing tree and the full moon... it's just like my dream. In the dream, unicorns would gather around an illuminating tree, basking in the soothing glow of the full moon. They would pass on celestial wisdom while putting out a loving energy that spread through the moonlight and touched the earth."

The group listened with close attention, transfixed by Lily's revelation. There was no denying the relationship between her dream and the fantastical event taking place above them. They appeared to have crossed over into the mysterious worlds they had only imagined as dreams and reality seemed to have merged.

Sara's voice entered the discourse, her tone filled with amazement. "Perhaps your dreams served as a conduit, a bridge that allowed us to access the unicorns' ancient wisdom. The energy they communicate through the moonlight may contain the secret to unlocking the magic within ourselves and restoring harmony to our world."

Giselle joined in, her eyes twinkling with playfulness and her laughter filling the air. "Or perhaps, just maybe, we are truly living in Lily's dream right now," she joked.

"True, perhaps we all dozed off on this deck," Jewell chuckled, "where the cool breeze caressed our faces, and the moonlight enchanted us."

The bunch burst out laughing, their joyous laughter booming through the night.

Unraveling the Forgotten Past

"Princess Acacia, Princess Acacia, Acacia..." Hank murmured, the name echoing in his head. "It sounds so familiar," he whispered, his voice tinged with shock and perplexity. As the puzzle pieces fell into place, Hank was overcome with emotion, forcing him to remove his t-shirt in a rush. Surprised eyes widened as he said, "This can't be real."

A startling insight washed over him as he looked at the scarification scars on his left chest and then at the necklace clasped in his palm. The marks and the necklace seemed inextricably linked as if they held the key to unlocking the riddles before him.

The gang was taken aback by Hank's sudden movement, their eyes widening in astonishment as they sat up straight, captivated by the unfolding scene. Curious and anticipating, they watched as Hank unveiled the hidden treasure on his left chest—a round scarification pattern adorned with ancient symbols. The intricate markings seemed to come alive, each sign weaving a tale of its own, carrying the weight of a forgotten past.

The deck fell into a reverent silence as the gang absorbed the sight before them. Like an ancient manuscript etched upon his skin, Hank's scarification held the echoes of a bygone era. The symbols spoke a long-forgotten language, whispering secrets and stories of ancient wisdom and power.

In the presence of this profound revelation, the air seemed charged with an esoteric atmosphere. The gang couldn't help but feel they were on the precipice of uncovering something extraordinary, a hidden connection to a realm beyond their wildest imaginations.

As they stared at the scarification, their minds began to race with questions. What did the symbols represent? What stories did they hold? And most importantly, what significance did they have for Hank and their shared journey?

The gang's astonishment lingered, each member lost in their own thoughts, trying to grasp the magnitude of this newfound revelation. They could sense that this scarification was more than scars on the skin—it was a portal to a forgotten world. This key unlocked the door to untold secrets and untamed magic.

"This scarification has the mark of ancient magic," Sara yelled, her voice full of wonder and realization. "Are you a descendant of the fabled ancient magician?" Sara asked incredulously.

Hank paused for a while before replying, "I'm

afraid so," with a mix of uncertainty and realization in his voice. "Since my parents passed away the year I had this scarification, I have avoided those ancient teachings. And I used to hear a tale from my grandma about a unicorn princess named Acacia. As a young boy, I was reluctant to listen. I didn't know why she would tell me a princess tale, especially right before bed. After that, she would recite a spell." Hank's voice became halting and confused with nostalgia.

All eyes moved to Hank, and a palpable suspense descended upon the group. He looked at the back of his necklace, which contained an inscription—an ancient spell—with a mixture of uncertainty and curiosity. He was overwhelmed by the gravity of this revelation and struggled to comprehend what he saw.

Hank muttered, "The spell... it's right here, on the back of this necklace," his voice trembling with shock. His thoughts were racing as he used his fingertip to trace the carved lines as this realization's consequences. There was no denying the relationship between the narratives of Princess Acacia, the tales told to him by his grandmother, and the mystical symbols inscribed on his chest and necklace.

The gang stood in awe, their eyes fixed on the necklace, as the weight of Hank's revelation settled upon them. It seemed the secrets of an ancient world had unveiled themselves, linking Hank's past, present, and magical realms that appeared to have converged upon their lives.

In this extraordinary discovery, Hank's mind raced with questions, his thoughts whirling with emotions. The significance of the scarification, the connection to Princess Acacia, and the revelation of the spell on the necklace overwhelmed him. He found himself at the crossroads of disbelief and acceptance, grappling with the enigmatic forces that had guided his journey.

The gang remained in silence, absorbing the weight of Hank's revelations. The puzzle pieces were slowly falling into place, and the extraordinary nature of their day seemed to surpass mere coincidence.

"It's really that simple, guys," G.T. added, his tone light but firm. "Let's bring together everything we discovered today. Our mission is simple — liberating Princess Acacia with a stone and bringing unicorn magic back to the world. Not to mention the fact that we now have a magician and a spell. But more than ever, I'm convinced I'm a part of Lily's dream now. The coincidences we've witnessed in just one day... It's all just too phenomenal to be true. I must be dreaming, or my mind is playing tricks on me."

Moon Rock

Giselle's voice rang out, filled with excitement and intrigue, as she pointed towards Hank's necklace. "Hank, look! The moonlight falls directly on the stone of your necklace. It's illuminating it in a peculiar way," she clamored.

Hank's eyes widened in astonishment as he gazed down at the necklace. The moonlight bathed the stone, casting an ethereal glow that seemed to bring the pendant to life. "That's incredible," he whispered, his voice filled with wonder. "It seems the moonlight is drawn to this stone."

Jewell leaned in closer, her eyes scrutinizing the stone. "Wait, it's not just the moonlight," she said. "The stone itself emits a subtle, mellow glow. It appears like a light source is located deep within, creating this intriguing radiance."

The gang gathered around, their attention fixed on the necklace and its enigmatic glow. They were captivated by the ethereal sight before them, a fusion of celestial light and inner luminescence.

"The stone seems to hold a secret," Lily speculated, her voice barely above a whisper.

"Would it be the stone related to Princess

Acacia?" Sara inquired, her voice complete with curiosity as she approached Hank.

"In my dream, the stone appeared hidden under the sea," Lily explained.

G.T. nodded in agreement and added his ideas. "Perhaps someone discovered it on the beach," he reasoned.

Giselle switched her gaze to Hank, her eyes glowing with eagerness. "Hank, did your grandma mention anything about the stone in the letter she left you?" she inquired.

Hank hesitated for a moment, contemplating his response. "I haven't had a chance to read the letter yet," he admitted, his voice tinged with regret. The weight of the unopened letter intensified, its contents holding the potential to unlock the secrets they sought.

A shared sense of anticipation filled the air as the group realized that the letter held the missing piece of the puzzle—a piece that could bring them closer to uncovering the truth about Princess Acacia and the stone that had the key to awakening her.

"Guys!" Wild pointed urgently toward the vast ocean as his voice quivered with a fierce mix of amazement and dread. "This is so unbelievable."

The group's senses were momentarily overtaken by a sight that defied all preconceived notions, and their eyes widened in absolute bewilderment.

A breathtaking spectacle unfolded before their eyes as lights resembling glistening diamonds' radiance flickered upon the ocean's surface. The ethereal glow danced and shimmered, casting a spellbinding illumination that transformed the water into a sea of sparkling enchantment. The play of light upon the waves created an illusion of a vast treasure of countless diamonds scattered across the surface, radiating a brilliance that left them awe-inspired.

Fergus's attention turned to Wild's voice, filled with a compelling blend of curiosity and anxiety. "You're right," he said, his gaze drawn to the captivating reflection of the lights on the ocean's surface. "The way those lights reflect the glow... it seems they contain the essence of a diamond, infused with the enchantment of moonlight."

The collective breath of the gathering froze in their throats as they gasped at the exquisite sight, fascinated by the shimmering lights that mirrored the splendor of a starry diamond enveloped in the brilliant embrace of the golden moonlight.

The group was overwhelmed with wonder and fascination as their eyes remained riveted on the incoming wave of gigantic diamond-like lights. The glow seemed to float through the water quickly, defying their massive size restrictions.

"Look, it's drawing closer to us!" said Giselle, her voice quivering with excitement. "But how exactly? What eerie force could direct such a majestic and radiant light?"

Anxiety grabbed their chests as Hank's warning pierced the air, "Oh no, it's a colossal wave!"

Panic coursed through their veins as they desperately clutched to the wreckage of their boat, but their attempts were hopeless. The wave slammed against them, hurling them into the whirling depths of the sea.

As the colossal wave crashed upon them, their bodies were hurled into the swirling depths of the sea. Disoriented and surrounded by a tumultuous maelstrom, they fought against the relentless currents that threatened to consume them.

Their world turned into a chaotic maelstrom of water in that critical moment. Disoriented and struggling against the powerful currents, they fought to regain their bearings. Yet, amidst the turmoil, a glimmer of hope emerged.

Beneath the surface, a breathtaking scene unfolded. The radiant glow of the diamond permeated the water, casting a luminous enchantment upon their surroundings. The ocean embraced their presence, guiding them gently with an unseen force, seeming like answering a call from the depths of their souls.

They were swimming in awe and wonder when they spotted the diamond's ethereal light carving a brilliant trail across the deep waters. The diamond light seemed to have mystical power, guiding them to an undiscovered destination known only via whispered legends and old tales.

A fascinating world of wonder was revealed by their watery journey. They came across an incredible variety of aquatic life, many of which appeared in iridescent hues that complemented the diamond's brilliant radiance. They were joined by graceful life forms that danced in a symphony of marine magic, their movements a tribute to the magnificent environment they lived in.

They fell deeper, attentively following the diamond's guiding light. The ocean revealed hidden wonders, such as an exceptional coral reef alive with brilliant marine flora and wildlife. Schools of bioluminescent fish illuminated their route, their bodies pulsing with a delicate, ethereal radiance, as if nature welcomed them.

And then, in the distance, an awe-inspiring sight greeted their eyes—a massive underwater city adorned with architectural wonders that seemed to merge seamlessly with the very essence of the ocean. The open structures reached toward the moonlit surface, their ethereal beauty a testament to the civilization that once thrived within these submerged walls.

The city streets were adorned with a mesmerizing display of sculptures, each intricately crafted to resemble rarely seen aquatic creatures and galactic planet orbit symbols. These extraordinary sculptures depicted fantastical beings that seemed to exist at the intersection of the earthly and cosmic realms.

Their forms were a harmonious fusion of mystical aquatic life and celestial wonders, capturing cosmic connections and events' essence. These stellar symbols, etched into the sculptures, hinted at cosmic events and connections, weaving a tale of the stars and their influence on the underwater realm. The sculptures shimmered with a diamond-like luminescence, casting an ethereal glow that illuminated the streets and brought the cosmic mysteries to life.

The haunting notes of far-off music swirled through the undersea, resonating with mellow energy transcending time. It was as though the melodies contained the echoes of antiquated wisdom, echoing the mysteries of vanished civilizations and cosmic alignments. The heavenly sounds mesmerized the group, their hearts moved by the deep linkages between the celestial and watery worlds.

Combining the intricate sculptures and the celestial melodies created a mystical ambiance that permeated the underwater city. It was a place where the earthly and the cosmic boundaries intertwined, inviting those who ventured within to explore the depths of the universe and unravel the cosmic tapestry that bound all things together.

As they immersed themselves in the ethereal beauty of the underwater city, a sense of wonder enfolded the group.

"Are... we... dead?" Wild couldn't help but inquire, his voice trembling with wonder. "Is this what heaven looks like?" The words hung in the water, echoing with curiosity and wonder.

With a radiant smile, Lily responded to Wild's query, "This is beyond amazing. It feels like stepping into a realm where dreams entwine with reality seamlessly." Her voice conveyed enchantment it seemed she had been here before.

"This place... I've been here before." Hank said. His eyes glistened with familiarity. "This is where I first met the unicorns." He spoke with a hint of nostalgia and a firm conviction that their present reality was extraordinary.

With his heart thoroughly moved by the enchanted surroundings, G.T. said, "I still believe we are inside Lily's dream. That's why we can talk to each other underwater."

Enthralled by the beauty all around her, Giselle couldn't help but say, "This is finer than any fantasy I could have dreamed. I can feel the water embracing me, and when the gentle radiance of the diamond touches my spirit, my heart fills with gratitude."

As they ventured deeper into the enchanting underwater city, anticipation filled the group. They marveled at the intricately carved sculptures and the melodies that permeated the water, guiding them further into the heart of the mystical realm.

Suddenly, Giselle's voice rang out, filled with surprise and delight. "Listen!" she shouted, her eyes widening with astonishment. "Lily, it's your song! The one you sang in front of the Rainbow Waterfall!" The familiar melody echoed through the underwater expanse, blending harmoniously with the gentle radiance from a magnificent waterfall ahead of them.

Lily's heart skipped a beat as she recognized the melodic strains. "Yes, it is!" Lily exclaimed, her voice filled with excitement and wonder. The music carried a transcendent power, resonating with the very essence of the diamond's glow and infusing its surroundings with vibrant energy.

The Celestial Symphony

Drawn by the enchanting melody, the group swam toward the source of the sound, their anticipation mounting with each stroke through the crystalline waters. As they approached the majestic waterfall, their eyes widened in astonishment at the scene that unfolded before them.

Emerging from a tiny, unassuming rough rock, a radiant glow emanated with dazzling brilliance. Above the diamond ray, a group of giant marine creatures floated gracefully, their majestic forms swaying and twirling in perfect harmony with the rhythmic patterns of the light. Their ethereal voices rose and fell, weaving a mesmerizing symphony that echoed through the underwater city.

Beneath the rock, golden waves flowed in a mesmerizing dance, their movement mirroring the melodic chant of the giant creatures. The waves seemed to possess a sentient quality as though they were sentient beings responding to the call of the music. They rose and fell, creating a captivating display of fluid motion that resonated with the hearts of the on-looking group. Eyes wide with awe and wonder, the group felt an undeniable connection to this extraordinary scene.

Hank's mind was filled with fascination and intrigue as they marveled at the enchanting spectacle. The giant marine creatures' majestic presence and ethereal dance reminded him of ancient legends and stories passed down by fishermen for generations.

"Are they The Doga?" Hank whispered in a shallow voice, almost afraid to disrupt the magical harmony before him. The legends spoke of mythical beings known as The Doga, ancient guardians of the ocean depths, said to possess unimaginable wisdom and power.

As they drew nearer to the radiant rock and

immersed themselves in its otherworldly glow, a profound transformation began to unfold. The diamond ray, its luminous power intensifying, seemed to radiate a magnetic force that pulled them closer. Gradually, the swirling portal opened before them, revealing a vast expanse where a galaxy unfolded in all its cosmic splendor.

Eyes wide with astonishment, the group was suspended amid a celestial tapestry. Countless stars twinkled with ethereal radiance, painting the cosmic canvas with vibrant hues and shimmering patterns. Nebulas swirled in kaleidoscopic beauty, their colors shifting and merging like the strokes of an artist's brush.

The grandeur of the scene before them was awe-inspiring. They could feel the cosmic energies pulsating through their very beings as if they had become one with the fabric of the universe. Time seemed to stand still as they floated within this cosmic symphony, their senses heightened and their spirits uplifted by the sheer magnitude of the cosmic dance around them.

As they gazed upon the celestial marvels, they realized they were witnessing the intricate interconnectedness of the cosmos. Galaxies spiraled and collided, giving birth to new stars and planets.

Heavenly bodies moved in orchestrated harmony, guided by unseen cosmic forces. It was a testament to the vastness and interconnectedness of the universe, a reminder that they were part of something much more significant than themselves.

They felt a deep sense of purpose and belonging within this celestial realm. Their guide through this cosmic voyage, the diamond ray, seemed to pulse with a gentle invitation. It beckoned them to explore the mysteries and wonders of the universe, to unlock the secrets within the depths of the cosmic expanse.

With hearts brimming with excitement and curiosity, they propelled themselves forward, passing through the swirling portal and into the cosmic embrace. As they ventured deeper into the galaxy, the ethereal melodies of the marine creatures accompanied their journey, intertwining with the divine rhythms that resonated throughout the cosmos.

As they ventured deeper into the cosmic expanse, surrounded by the galaxy's breathtaking beauty, the group felt an overwhelming sense of connection and belonging. The celestial wonders unfolding before them resonated with a familiarity that touched their souls.

"This is why people say we're from the stars," Sara said in an awe-filled voice that resounded in everyone's hearts." I can even feel the cosmos within me."

Lily, moved to tears by the profound beauty surrounding them, nodded in agreement. "I feel the same," she whispered, her voice filled with reverence and joy. "A sense of home washes over me as if I had returned to where I originated."

Wild, reflecting on the cosmic revelations, added his insight. "No wonder those with near-death experiences often express reluctance to return. They had caught a glimpse of this divine panorama, a place that transcends our earthly existence."

Each group member was overcome by their unique wonderment in this celestial voyage. They were immersed in a realm where time lost its hold, where the boundaries of their perceptions expanded beyond measure. It was a moment of profound clarity, where they glimpsed the infinite possibilities that awaited them in the vastness of the cosmos.

As they continued their cosmic journey, they embraced the cosmic truth that they were stardust beings, intricately woven into the cosmic fabric. They realized that they were more than just physical beings; they were luminous souls forever connected to the cosmic dance of creation.

As the group continued their cosmic journey,

their senses heightened with anticipation. Fergus's voice, filled with excitement, interrupted the profound silence, "Look!"

All eyes turned towards Fergus, their gazes fixed on the sight that had captured his attention. In the distance, a celestial planet shimmered with an otherworldly glow. It beckoned to them, drawing them closer with its captivating radiance.

As they approached the planet, their awe deepened. A magnificent tree stood at the center, its branches reaching the heavens. Each branch was adorned with massive shining lights resembling leaves that glowed with an enchanting brilliance. Upon closer inspection, they realized that these lights took the form of majestic unicorns' horns, their ethereal presence illuminating the cosmic expanse.

Beneath the root of the luminous tree, a bright diamond light emanated with a brilliance that surpassed anything they had witnessed before. Its radiance danced with a mesmerizing allure, casting a kaleidoscope of colors that painted the cosmic landscape.

In the presence of this celestial spectacle, they felt a surge of cosmic energy coursing through their beings. The diamond light seemed to mirror the depths of their souls, igniting a profound sense of purpose and destiny within each of them.

They approached the tree with reverence, their hearts filled with a mix of awe and humility. As they stood beneath its luminous branches, they could sense the ancient wisdom and cosmic power that emanated from every fiber of its being.

Giselle's voice, barely above a whisper, broke the silence, "This is truly a place of cosmic magic. The tree, the unicorn lights, and the radiant diamond light beneath seem to hold the universe's secrets."

Lily's eyes shimmering with wonder, added, "This glowing tree seems a conduit, connecting us to the cosmic wisdom and astral light that flow through the universe. Its profound grace embraces us."

Each group member felt a deep resonance with the cosmic energies emanating from the tree. They understood that this luminous sanctuary was the key to unlocking the universe's deepest mysteries, offering them insights into their destinies.

Fergus gazed at his body and the other members of the group in astonishment. He held back his disbelief and shouted, "This is beyond my knowing. It seems this tree resonates with our DNA or spirit."

The group was in stunned silence as Fergus' words spread throughout this magical place. Everyone couldn't help but examine their body as they became aware of a mysterious shift. Their essence seemed to have fused with the very fabric of the celestial tree, their beings grew entangled with its brilliant branches. Their bodies were pumped with vibrant lights, energy that matched the tree's magnificent radiance.

Streams of radiant light coursed through their bodies as if they were being charged by the very source of illumination itself. They felt an undeniable unity with the tree, an intertwining of their beings with its profound cosmic energy.

☆

During their awe-inspiring experiences, Giselle's voice pierced through their trance. Her eyes widened with concern as she realized that Hank was nowhere to be found among them. "Where is Hank?" she exclaimed, her voice laced with worry and urgency.

The group's unity was momentarily disrupted as they frantically scanned the luminous expanse, searching for their dear friend. The realization that Hank was not among them struck the gang like a bolt of lightning, in an instant, they were drawn back through the swirling portal.

Their hearts raced as they scanned their surroundings, searching for any sign of Hank's presence near the enigmatic rock. A collective sigh of relief escaped their lips upon seeing Hank still in the presence of the mysterious rock.

However, something seemed amiss. Hank's face contorted with a mixture of resistance and discomfort as he bent his body, clutching his chest. Concern etched on their faces, the gang gathered around him, their voices filled with worry.

"Hank, are you all right?" Lily's voice trembled with concern as she reached out a hand toward him.

Hank was finally able to answer with a difficult but resolute exhale. His eyes showed a mixture of doubt and concern as he said, "When I approached the rock, it seemed to delve into the depths of my mind. The light shifted into a massive backdrop that projected my long-forgotten hidden story."

The group exchanged bewildered glances, their minds racing to comprehend the significance of Hank's experience. It seemed the light emanating from the rock had tapped into his very heart, unveiling the deepest wounds and memories. A shiver ran down their spines as they considered the implications of this profound interaction.

Jewell's understanding gaze softened as she reached out to touch Hank's shoulder, her voice filled with sincerity and compassion. "Hank, we are all here with you," she said, her words carrying a profound sense of empathy and unity.

The moment Hank felt Jewell's touch, a wave of comfort washed over him, and he could no longer resist the memories that flooded his mind. As if guided by an unseen force, the group was captivated by the vivid scenes playing out before them.

They watched as a young Hank, just eight years old, underwent a scarification tattoo, tears streaming down his face from the pain. His father sits beside him, a pillar of strength, offering his support and wisdom.

A gentle and wise voice emanated from Hank's father, filled with love and understanding. "I am here with you," his father said, his touch on Hank's shoulder grounding him in the present moment. "These scars will become a part of you, a reminder of the transformative power within. Every human carries scars throughout life, and it is how we embrace them that defines us." he came to a halt and peered lovingly at Hank.

"If you kept them hidden, they would turn into wounds that became deeper and heavier. Yet, once you're ready to face them, these scars will become a beacon of light leading you back to your true home."

Hank's father continued, speaking with profound wisdom in his voice. "Remember, you don't have to endure suffering like a warrior to be resilient.

Strength lies in recognizing and embracing them, for a true man doesn't hide his weaknesses. By acknowledging your scars and being authentic, your body becomes a physical shrine, honoring the experiences that shaped you, and reminding you of the resilience that flows through your veins."

While the gang was touched by Hank's story, the images shifted, revealing another painful chapter of his life. They witnessed the aftermath of a tragic accident in which Hank lost his parents. The young Hank, overwhelmed with grief, became numb to his emotions, burying his anger deep within. In a moment of anguish, he distanced himself from his ancestral origins and teaching, even changing his last name as he grew older.

As the memories unfolded, the weight of Hank's buried pains became palpable. The gathering stood in silent empathy, their hearts burdened with the awareness of his anguish.

Jewell's gentle voice broke the silence. "Hank, you've endured so much loss and pain," she said softly. "Your grief is never a sign of weakness. Instead, it's the tremendous love you kept for your parents."

Hank, his eyes gleaming with sorrow and determination, took a deep breath and embarked on self-discovery. He could no longer hide from his past or suppress his emotions. The diamond ray sensed his resolve and enveloped him in its ethereal embrace. Its shimmering light cascaded over his body, shedding the remnants of old wounds and infusing him with renewed life force.

As the rejuvenating energy penetrated his being, Hank's eyes widened in amazement. The diamond ray understood his commitment to confront his history and embrace his true self. In each passing moment, the weight of his burdens lessened. The oppression that had long plagued him began to lift, replaced by a profound sensation of liberation and inner strength.

The gang watched in awe as Hank's change unfolded before their eyes. His countenance became illuminated, his spirit alight with a newfound sense of purpose.

As the group marveled at Hank's remarkable transformation, Giselle's sharp observation pulled their attention back to the shining rock. Her voice carried a mix of excitement and realization as she declared, "I think this is the stone we've been searching for!"

Lily's voice echoed with certainty, "Yes, Giselle, this is the stone we've been seeking all along!"

Wild, still reeling from the revelation, asked,

"This is the stone?"

"How come we didn't notice it sooner?" Sara spoke up, her voice full of wonder, "It's strange how it slipped us until now."

"But, how do we release Princess Acacia from this rock?" G.T., ever focused on the mission at hand, remarked.

The cadence of the golden waves beneath the rock changed subtly, as though in response to the mention of Princess Acacia. The group's attention was quickly drawn to the changing motion as if to provide some indications, and their hearts were pounding with excitement.

"Hank!" the gang spoke in unison, their eyes fixed on him with a mixture of hope and trust. They knew that Hank's connection to the rock and his transformative journey held the key to unlocking the secrets of Princess Acacia's release.

"I am a marine biologist, not a sorcerer," Hank's embarrassment was palpable as he acknowledged his background as a marine biologist. He admitted, feeling a mix of inadequacy and uncertainty.

Hank was comforted by Sara's sympathetic and understanding voice when she said, "It's okay. Your career as a marine biologist must have a deeper relationship to the puzzles we're trying to solve. We have arrived here due to your research on the Mariana Trench."

In agreement, Jewell nodded, her eyes glistening with encouragement. "My grandmother used to say that our lives are intricately woven. Whatever choices we make, they always serve to bring us back to our true purpose."

G.T., with a glimmer of determination in his eyes, proposed a solution. "Maybe we should try the spell," he suggested.

Giselle's eyes sparkled with excitement as she added, "Yes, it might hold the key to unlocking the stone's secret."

Hank hesitated for a moment, not accustomed to practicing magic. "All right, it's worth a try," he finally agreed, mustering up his courage. With a clunky pronunciation, Hank began to recite the spell, stumbling over the unfamiliar words.

"*Ah... Kii ...Helu....Sa...* No, should be *Sawii Wuk..d. Ta.*"

The rest of the gang watched with bated breath, hoping for a miraculous change.

However, as the last syllables of the spell escaped Hank's lips, nothing visibly changed. The rock remained unchanged, and there was no sign of Princess Acacia's release. Disappointment flickered across their faces, but they refused to give up hope.

"We must not lose faith," Lily said, with a voice full of resolve.

Wild observed something odd when the group was debating how to cast the spell. His eyes widened in the revelation, "This is weird," he said. "When Hank says the spell, the golden waves come near!"

As the golden waves began to swirl and grow more intense, Giselle couldn't help but look around with a sly grin in her eyes. "Golden waves?" she joked, a wicked smile tugging at the corners of her mouth. "Perhaps mermaids are coming to greet us!"

The rest of the gang chuckled, their spirits lifted by Giselle's lighthearted remark. The atmosphere in the space became filled with a sense of joy and anticipation feeling like the underwater realm itself was joining in their excitement.

G.T., his determination undeterred, spoke up again. "Perhaps there's a specific intonation or rhythm to the spell that we haven't discovered yet," he suggested. "Let's try again, but this time, let's focus on the flow and cadence of the words."

"Hank, do you remember how your grandmother used to say it?" Sara inquired, her voice overflowing with enthusiasm.

Hank's eyes flashed with recognition as

childhood memories flooded his head. He remembered those enchanting nights spent by his grandmother's side, her vibrant tale, and how she became dramatically absorbed when reciting the spell. The epiphany hit him like a bolt of lightning. "I got it," he cried, his newfound clarity sweeping over him.

"Okay, let's give it another shot," with a fresh sense of mission, Hank said with a voice of determination. He took a deep breath and started the spell again, this time paying close attention to the melody and rhythm of the words, "*Ah Kii Helu Sawii Wukd Tai.*"

Everyone's eyes widened, fixated on the mesmerizing shimmer of the rock, as Hank recited the spell with newfound confidence. Time itself seemed to hold its breath as they anxiously awaited the outcome. However, with each passing moment, disappointment began to weave its way into their hearts. It seemed as though their collective efforts had been in vain, the elusive solution slipping through their fingertips.

While their minds churned with thoughts of what else could be done, the scarification mark, once a static symbol etched upon Hank's chest, suddenly awakened. It pulsated with a vibrant glow, resonating with the brilliance of the diamond light that bathed his body.

Wild, overwhelmed by a mix of awe and bewilderment, couldn't contain his astonishment. "What is happening here?" he yelled, his gaze locked onto Hank's enigmatic scarification.

Hank himself was equally taken aback, his fingertips grazing the scars, now imbued with the radiant essence of the diamond light.

"The light's dimensional patterns seem to embody a sacred geometry," speculated Sara, her voice tinged with an insatiable curiosity.

"But how do you explain the light coming from his body?" Giselle questioned, her eyes searching for deeper understanding.

"It appears to me that the light emanates from Hank's energy field," Fergus added, his voice carrying an air of reverence. "We are in a rare and exceptional energy vortex. What we are witnessing goes beyond the limitations of our normal physical eyes."

"People say the moment we shift our consciousness, our energy field adapts to match its frequency right away," Sara added, her words tinged with a sense of wonder. "Sounds also carry a frequency. It seems the spell was designed to unlock Hank's innate abilities, dormant until this very moment."

"Or perchance, the wooden necklace serves as a key, a passcode for unlocking the mysteries intertwined within," G.T. pondered aloud, his fingers delicately grasping Hank's necklace. As he attempted to align the wooden symbols with the ethereal lights emanating from Hank's scarification mark, a sudden surge of energy coursed through G.T.'s hand, freezing it in place.

Wide-eyed and bewildered, G.T. realized something profound had occurred. And in the next breathtaking moment, the rock embedded within the necklace detached itself, floating ever so gracefully toward the radiant rock with its ethereal diamond ray, as if guided by an invisible force.

A sense of awe and wonder filled the air as the two rocks merged, their energies intertwining in a mystical dance. In an instant, a blinding ray of light burst forth from the merged rocks, illuminating the entire underwater city. The opal walls reflected the diamond ray, causing the city to transform into a magnificent diamond metropolis. The once-subdued hues now sparkled with an otherworldly radiance, casting a breathtaking glow throughout the vast expanse.

As the stones merged, the giant marine creatures that had mesmerized the group with their graceful dance and song swam upwards, following the path of moonlight that pierced the water's surface. With a burst of joyous energy, their massive bodies leaped from the water, somersaulting and flipping in mid-air, their movements a testament to the pure ecstasy they felt in this extraordinary moment.

The Reborn Unicorn

As the giant marine creatures soared higher into the moonlit surface, the moonlight itself seemed to respond to their jubilant movements. It wrapped around their bodies like shimmering ribbons, casting a soft, ethereal glow that accentuated their every graceful twist and turn. The moonlight danced with them, creating a mesmerizing spectacle that seemed to defy the laws of gravity.

Each creature left behind a trail of sparkling stardust as they leaped and flipped in perfect synchronization. The stardust glittered and shimmered, forming intricate patterns in the night sky, like celestial fireworks that painted the darkness with bursts of cosmic radiance. The gang could feel the energy of the stardust tingling on their skin, an enchanting reminder of the magical connection between all living beings.

The moon itself seemed to smile down upon the spectacle, its gentle rays caressing the surface of the water as if in celebration. The reflection of the moonlight on the waves transformed the underwater city into a shimmering dreamscape, where every surface seemed to come alive with a luminous, otherworldly glow.

As the giant marine creatures twirled and spun, their movements became more fluid and effortless, as if they were guided by an invisible force. It was as if the moonlight had breathed life into their bodies, enhancing their natural grace and elegance. They created mesmerizing shapes in the air, their bodies intertwining and separating in a seamless ballet that spoke of harmony and unity.

The gang watched in awe as the creatures formed a colossal circle in the sky, their bodies glowing like constellations against the dark canvas. They radiated an aura of serenity and wisdom as if they were the keepers of ancient cosmic secrets. The celestial dance they performed carried messages encoded in their elegant motions, messages that could only be understood by those with open hearts and receptive souls.

As the grand celestial dance came to a close, a mystical transformation occurred before the astonished eyes of the gang. The giant marine creatures, their bodies aglow with radiant energy, began to metamorphose into magnificent, illuminating unicorns. Their sleek forms shimmered with an otherworldly light, and their eyes sparkled with ancient wisdom.

With a graceful leap, the unicorns descended back into the water, their glistening horns leading the way. They formed a majestic circle around the diamond ray rock, their presence creating a protective barrier of ethereal magic. The water around them seemed to come alive, swirling and shimmering with an iridescent glow.

The unicorns' hooves kicked the water, causing delicate ripples to spread throughout the underwater realm. These ripples carried a harmonious vibration, resonating with the very essence of the diamond ray and the interconnectedness of all life.

As the unicorns circled the rock, their manes, and tails fluttered like streams of stardust, casting a mesmerizing pattern of light and shadow on the sea bed. Their collective energy seemed to infuse the surroundings with a profound sense of tranquility and serenity.

Enchanting by the presence of the unicorns and their cosmic energy, the golden waves responded in harmony. They swelled and expanded, forming a protective barrier around the unicorns and the rock. The waves radiated a warm golden glow, intertwining with the luminescence of the unicorns' horns as if merging their powers to create an impenetrable shield.

The golden waves undulated gracefully, their gentle movements resembling a dance of celestial currents. They pulsed with a soothing rhythm, amplifying the sense of peace and security that enveloped the entire area. It was as if the ocean itself acknowledged the significance of the reborn unicorn and joined forces to safeguard the precious diamond and the cosmic energies it embodied.

The gang stood in reverent silence, aware of the sacredness of this moment. They could feel the gentle pulse of the unicorns' magic radiating through the water, embracing them with a deep sense of belonging. The unicorns, guardians of the diamond ray's power, seemed to communicate a message of unity and harmony that transcended language and touched the core of their souls.

With a synchronized movement, the unicorns lowered their heads, their spiraling horns glowing with an intensified iridescent brilliance. Luminous energy emanated from their horns, intertwining with the radiant glow of the diamond ray. The combined brilliance created a dazzling spectacle as if the very fabric of the underwater world had been woven with strands of pure light.

The gang, drawn by an irresistible force, stepped closer to the unicorns and the diamond ray rock. As they approached, they could feel the pulse of the cosmic energy coursing through their veins, connecting them to the ancient wisdom and infinite possibilities of the universe.

With each passing moment, the shining rock began to undergo a wondrous transformation. Colors danced and shifted across its surface as if a kaleidoscope of cosmic energy was being channeled into its very core. The rock seemed to come alive, shimmering with a luminous brilliance that surpassed anything the gang had ever witnessed.

As the metamorphosis continued, a breathtaking sight unfolded before their eyes. From the collective light of the unicorns, a magnificent creature emerged, its form radiant and resplendent. A beautiful unicorn, adorned with a coat as white as the purest snow and a mane and tail that flowed like liquid stardust, stood before them. Its eyes, filled with wisdom and kindness, met theirs as if acknowledging their presence.

This reborn unicorn, awaken from the collective essence of the unicorns, emanated an aura of profound magic and power. It carried within it the wisdom of ages, the secrets of the cosmos, and the ability to guide and protect those who dared to venture into the realms of enchantment.

As the reborn unicorn stood before them, a shimmering diamond adorned its forehead, casting a mesmerizing glow. The diamond, radiant and ethereal, seemed to contain the very essence of the diamond ray itself.

The gang marveled at the sight of the diamond on the unicorn's forehead, sensing its significance. They understood that this precious gem was more than mere decoration; it represented a sacred symbol of wisdom and divine guidance. It was a beacon of light, illuminating their path and reminding them of the cosmic purpose that had brought them together.

With a graceful gesture, the reborn unicorn inclined its head, inviting the gang to approach. They stepped forward, their hearts brimming with awe and gratitude, as they stood in the presence of this majestic creature. They could sense silent communication, an exchange of energy and understanding that transcended words.

Lily, her voice filled with wonder and reverence, dared to ask the question that lingered in everyone's mind, "Are you, Princess Acacia?"

As if in response to her inquiry, the unicorn's diamond light radiated from its forehead, casting a luminous glow that enveloped the surroundings. In a breathtaking transformation, the unicorn's majestic form dissolved, giving way to the appearance of a goddess-like human. Her hair shimmered like a cascade of stars, and her eyes glistened with crystalline clarity. She exuded an ethereal presence, a fusion of grace and power.

The group stood in awe, realizing that they were indeed in the presence of the legendary Princess Acacia herself. The air crackled with anticipation as the other unicorns also underwent a miraculous metamorphosis, assuming human forms that mirrored their majestic essence.

Each member of the group was captivated by the divine radiance emanating from these light warriors. The male and female figures stood tall and resolute, embodying a harmonious blend of strength and compassion. Their eyes held a depth of wisdom that spoke of ancient knowledge, and their presence exuded an aura of protection and guidance.

Lily and the gang were struck with awe and disbelief, realizing the profound connection that bound them to Princess Acacia. It was as if the threads of their destinies had been intricately woven together, guided by the cosmic forces that permeated their lives. The realization that their journey had been orchestrated by a higher power filled their hearts with a profound sense of purpose and wonder.

Princess Acacia, her voice a melodic harmony, spoke with an air of regality, her words resonating with the weight of ancient wisdom. "Yes, Lily," she confirmed, her gaze filled with understanding. "I am Acacia, the guardian of cosmic wisdom and the bearer of the Source Diamond Ray. It is I who weaves the enchanting melody of the unicorns into your dreams, guiding you on this extraordinary journey of discovery and purpose."

Acacia, her presence radiant and majestic, extended her hand toward Lily and the gang. "Your paths have converged with mine for a very special reason," she spoke, her voice resonating with ethereal power. "Together, we are destined to unlock the ancient wisdom that lies dormant within the sacred Chamber of Eternity."

Her eyes shining with a mix of astonishment and gratitude, Lily stepped forward, reaching out to clasp Acacia's hand. The rest of the gang followed suit, forming a circle of unity and determination. They were prepared to accept their connected fates and set out on a journey that would bring out their inner fortitude and real calling.

Acacia's wise gaze turned towards Hank, a glimmer of recognition in her eyes. "Hank," she said, her voice carrying a hint of mystery, "More secrets are waiting to be revealed for you. Our paths shall cross once again, and the unfolding of your destiny shall bring forth even greater wonders."

As Hank locked eyes with Acacia, a profound connection was forged, and he felt a surge of mystical energy coursing through his veins. In that fleeting moment, something magical was activated within Hank, awakening a dormant power that would guide him on his unique journey of self-discovery.

☆

Acacia's gaze shifted towards the shimmering golden waves, and a warm smile graced her face. "My dear merfolk and Orville," she spoke with a reverence that resonated throughout the chamber. In response to her words, the golden shields surrounding the merfolk and Orville dissipated, revealing their true forms.

The gang stood in awe, their eyes wide with wonder as they beheld the majestic mermaids and the unique seahorse Orville. Each of them exuded an aura of ocean wisdom and innate power, their presence a testament to the hidden depths of the underwater realm.

Wild, his eyes wide with disbelief, shouted, "My god, they're real! They're mermaids!"

The gang stood in awe, their senses overwhelmed by the sheer wonder of the moment.

G.T., catching a glimpse of a merman among the enchanting beings, interjected, "And merman too!"

"More than that, a giant seahorse, too!" Sara exclaimed in a hushed tone, her eyes widening in astonishment.

They couldn't believe their eyes as they gazed upon the legendary creatures before them, their tails swaying gracefully in the currents, their ethereal beauty casting a spell of enchantment.

Amidst the profound astonishment, Wild's voice dropped to a hushed tone as he stared at one of the mermaids. "She looks so familiar," he murmured, a hint of recognition lingering in his words. It was as if a long-lost memory was on the precipice of resurfacing, tantalizingly close yet elusive.

The gang found themselves unable to tear their

eyes away from the mesmerizing sight. The mermaids and merman exuded an undeniable aura, captivating and soothing at the same time. In their presence, the space seemed to carry a sense of tranquility and wonder, seeming like the secrets of the ocean whispered through the currents surrounding them.

As the gentle waves caressed their aquatic forms, the mermaids and merman moved with a grace that seemed effortless as if they were at one with the ebb and flow of the sea. It was a captivating display of beauty and mystique, drawing the gang deeper into a world they had only dreamed of before.

Acacia's voice carried a tone of deep respect and gratitude as she addressed the merfolk and Orville. "Please convey my greatest regards and heartfelt gratitude to Queen Meridia for her unwavering protection throughout all this time," she spoke, her voice carrying a sense of reverence and camaraderie.

The mermaids and Orville, in their ethereal beauty, nodded in acknowledgment, their eyes sparkling with a shared sense of purpose.

Racing Against Darkness

While Acacia expressed her gratitude to the merfolk, a sudden change enveloped the underwater city. The once-illuminated surroundings began to dim, casting a veil of darkness over their location. Confusion and concern filled the air as the gang exchanged worried glances, their senses heightened by the palpable shift in the surrounding.

In the middle of the rising discomfort, Hank, ever alert, stated his insight. "The moonlight...it appears to be covered by gloomy clouds," he observed, his voice full of anxiety.

As the underwater city grew darker, an unsettling silence settled in, broken only by the distant sound of shifting currents. The gang, feeling the weight of the encroaching darkness, found themselves on edge, their instincts urging them to be vigilant.

Amidst the chaos, Acacia and her unicorn companions shared a momentary exchange of hesitant glances, their eyes reflecting the gravity of the situation. The merfolk and Orville, attuned to the shifting energy, activated their shimmering shields once again, cocooning themselves in a radiant golden aura of protection. The waves of light danced around them, shielding them from the impending darkness.

Before anyone could react, a cascade of swirling ashes, like ethereal snowflakes, began to descend upon the once-vibrant underwater city. The once-colorful fish and vibrant corals faded into a desolate monochromatic haze, their brilliance snuffed out by the encroaching gloom. The ground beneath their feet trembled with increasing intensity, causing the gang to clutch onto each other for stability, their faces etched with a mix of fear and disorientation.

"It seems... an earthquake," G.T. shouted, his voice barely audible amidst the growing chaos. The walls of the city groaned and cracked, giving way to the powerful force of the shifting tectonic plates.

Hank, driven by instinct and guided by an inner knowing, took charge. "We must find a way out," he declared. With a steady hand, he guided the group through the crumbling corridors, seeking a path to safety amid the collapsing infrastructure.

The gang pressed forward, their hearts pounding with a blend of fear and adrenaline. The once-familiar surroundings had transformed into a labyrinth of debris and darkness, each step fraught with uncertainty. As they navigated the treacherous terrain, their connection grew stronger, their trust in one another unwavering.

With each passing moment, the urgency of their escape intensified. They could feel the weight of the earth shifting beneath them, the tremors growing more pronounced with each step. Darkness enveloped their surroundings, making it nearly impossible to discern a clear path forward. Panic threatened to consume them, but just as despair began to settle in, a glimmer of hope appeared. Through the murky darkness, they saw the golden waves drawing near, their ethereal glow casting a faint light on their path.

"It's mermaids!" Giselle exclaimed, her voice filled with elation and awe. The sight of the mystic creatures filled her with a renewed sense of hope and excitement.

"Let's follow them," Wild said, his voice full of relief and resolve.

With no other choices in sight, the gang went on, following the golden waves that led them through the crumbling city's labyrinthine ruins. The remains of the once-thriving metropolis seemed to spring to life with an old mysticism as if the mermaids themselves were guiding them on a sacred journey through the ruins of a long-forgotten civilization.

Navigating the treacherous terrain, they relied solely on their instincts and the guiding light before them. The sound of rushing water grew louder, indicating the proximity of a waterfall.

The mermaids, sensing their responsibility to protect Acacia, informed the group that they could only escort them thus far.

"We must go back for Princess Acacia now," Nadia explained, her voice filled with both determination and concern.

The group recognized and thanked them for their brief presence. A sudden revelation struck Wild like lightning as the gang struggled with the gravity of their situation.

"I think I know the way out," he said, his voice full of newfound assurance. He swam towards the roaring waterfall's heart without hesitation. The rest of the group had no choice but to follow his intuition.

Their bodies propelled by a mixture of fear and determination, swam against the powerful current of the waterfall. The water cascaded around them, its roar echoing in their ears. The darkness seemed impenetrable, but they pressed on, their trust in Wild's guidance unwavering.

As they ventured deeper into the waterfall, a glimmer of light beckoned them forward. Gradually, the darkness gave way to a breathtaking sight—an underwater cavern bathed in an iridescent glow. The walls shimmered with luminescent crystals, casting a soft translucent light that revealed the path ahead.

Drawing nearer, they witnessed a mesmerizing spectacle unfolding before their eyes. An opening at the top of the cavern revealed a sliver of the outside world, and the sky beyond was ablaze with vibrant hues. The sun was on the brink of rising from the horizon, casting its radiant glow into the depths of the underwater realm.

As the gang emerged from the luminous cavern and swam towards the surface, a sense of familiarity washed over them. Lily, her eyes filled with wonder, looked around and sensed something deeply familiar.

"It looks familiar," she exclaimed, her voice tinged with awe. "I feel like I've been here before."

A mischievous smile spread across Wild's face as he swam toward the water's edge. "Yes, you have!" he laughed, his voice filled with joy. "We are home." With a swift movement, he leaped out of the water, landing gracefully on the ground.

Confusion and disbelief filled the others as they followed suit, their bodies dripping with the remnants of their underwater adventure.

"How do you know it's connected?" Hank asked, his voice a mix of curiosity and disbelief.

With a knowing expression on his face, Wild turned to face his friends. He said, "Remember this morning, Lily sang at the Rainbow Waterfall," he reminded them. "This is the very place where our journey began."

As the gang stepped out of the water and looked around, their eyes widened in astonishment. It was indeed the same Rainbow Waterfall that had mesmerized them earlier. The lush surroundings, the vibrant flora, and the cascading water formed a scene straight out of their memories.

G.T.'s excitement erupted as he shouted, "It is the Rainbow Waterfall! The place where Lily's enchanting voice echoed this morning."

The gang exchanged glances, a shared realization dawning upon them. Their journey had come full circle, leading them back to the very place where it had all started.

Fergus paused for a moment, his brow furrowing in deep thought. Suddenly, a spark of recollection ignited within him, and he turned to Wild. "Wait a minute, what did you see this morning? You mentioned something about this place before we headed back to the cottage," he questioned, curiosity tinged with anticipation in his voice.

Wild gently tapped Fergus on the shoulder, a smile playing on his lips. "I saw a mermaid swimming beneath the waterfall this morning," he confessed. "But I was afraid you would laugh at me if I mentioned it." He glanced at Giselle, who stared at him in disbelief.

"She is one of them?" Giselle couldn't fathom the connection, her eyes searching Wild's face for confirmation.

"Yes," Wild replied, his laughter bubbling up. "This is totally beyond my wildest imagination!"

In their astonishment, a sense of serendipity filled the air. It was as if the universe had guided their every step, weaving a tapestry of connections that defied logic. They marveled at the synchronicity that had brought them back to this sacred location, where their destinies had been set into motion.

As the realization sank in, a renewed sense of purpose stirred within the gang. They had returned to the starting point, but they were not the same individuals who had embarked on this journey. They had grown, learned, and discovered truths that had transformed them.

With a shared determination, the gang looked at each other, their eyes shining with newfound resolve. The Chamber of Eternity awaited them, and they were ready to face the mysteries that lay within. The bonds of friendship had deepened, and the strength of their collective spirit would guide them through the challenges yet to come.

.Thirteen.
TiTi's Letter

13

*A*fter resting from the magical adventure, the coast was painted with the tranquil hues of the sunset, casting a warm golden glow upon the waters. Hank walked slowly towards the shore, his mind a whirlwind of emotions as he tried to sink in what had transpired the night before, and the incredible journey that had unfolded over the past several years.

He gazed out at the vast expanse of the ocean, his lifetime love, where he had once lost his promising career as a marine biologist. Yet, in return, he had discovered a treasure beyond his wildest dreams—a treasure that unlocked the greater pieces of the mystical puzzles surrounding him.

As Hank stood there, the ocean waves seemed to whisper words of understanding. The water lapped at his feet like a gentle cradle, soothing his weary soul. He found a cozy spot on the sandy shore and settled down, clutching the letter from his grandma—a letter he had been reluctant to open, fearing the emotions it would unleash.

Inhaling deeply, he finally mustered the courage to unseal the letter. The parchment felt smooth and delicate in his hands, carrying with it a weight of wisdom and love. As he began to read the words written by his beloved grandma, the memories of her presence flooded his mind.

"*My dear Hank,*" the letter began,

"*As you read these words, I want you to feel the depth of my love, even beyond the physical realm. Death is not an end, but a profound transformation—a beckoning for our souls to reunite with the very essence of our being.*

It is a call to reconnect with the land that once

cradled us, our ancestors who paved the paths we walk upon, our loved ones who accompanied us during precious moments, and the eternal source of light that guides us on our journey."

Tears welled up in Hank's eyes as he felt his grandma's love enveloping him through her words. She continued,

"In you, I see a remarkable gift—a bridge that spans the realms of the known and the unknown, the visible and the invisible. The moment the scarification mark adorned your skin, it became evident that you were destined to honor our ancestral lineage and breathe life back into the magic that flows through our heritage. It stands as a radiant symbol, a testament to your sacred role as a guardian of the mystic."

As the sun dipped below the horizon, casting a warm, rosy glow across the waters, Hank felt a sense of peace settling within him. The ocean seemed to murmur in agreement as if echoing his grandmother's words. It was as if the sea itself acknowledged his unique connection to the enchanted world.

With each passing line, the letter unveiled the truth behind his remarkable journey, the significance of the magical stone, and the destiny that awaited him. Hank's heart quickened with anticipation as he continued to read.

"There was a time, magic flowed effortlessly through every living creature on our beloved planet. The cosmos and the Earth were harmoniously intertwined, and humans lived in unity with celestial beings, elements, fairies, unicorns, dragons, and all the magical wonders that enchanted our world.

Yet, a shadow fell upon us—a time of darkness when the brilliance within began to dim. It was during this era that Princess Acacia, the embodiment of diamond light from unicorn's kingdom, tragically had her life force bound within a stone. Fate, in its mysterious ways, guided the stone to the ocean's depths, where it was struck and split in two. One fragment remained lost beneath the waves, while the other was lovingly fashioned into the necklace you now hold.

It is as if the universe is whispering to us, reminding us of the significance of unity. To bring back the magic that has been obscured, one must venture beyond the confines of the known, embracing the mysteries of the invisible realms. It is a journey of shedding old beliefs, like a snake shedding its skin, and stepping bravely into the liminal spaces of transformation.

To awaken Princess Acacia, one has to uncover the diamond that lies within his own heart, all illusions must be transcended. You must see beyond the veils of deception, for the diamond reflects only truth. In becoming the diamond, you must release all impurities and fears, passing through the trials that test your courage and resilience.

In this present moment, you stand as a link in an unbroken chain—a bridge between the wisdom of your ancestors and the dreams of future generations. You are here and now, connected to the lineage that courses through your veins. Remember, my dear, you are never alone. Every step you take, every challenge you face, is intertwined with the collective spirit of our shared existence.

Embrace the magnitude of this journey, my beloved grandchild, for it is one of profound transformation and discovery. Trust in the guidance of your ancestors, the whispers of the unseen forces that surround you, and the essence of your being. Let your heart guide you, for it holds the wisdom of countless generations.

As you navigate the trials and illusions that lie ahead, remember that you are a diamond in the making. Allow the light within you to shine brilliantly, illuminating the path not only for yourself but for all who long to rediscover the magic that lies dormant within their souls.

With eternal love and unwavering belief in your incredible journey,

Grandma TiTi."

As he reached the end of the letter, Hank's eyes brimmed with tears of gratitude and hope. With the letter clasped tightly to his chest, Hank watched the ocean waves dance under the setting sun. He felt a renewed sense of purpose and determination. The magical adventure had only just begun, and he was ready to embrace every challenge, unlock the magic within himself, and restore the connection between the visible and the invisible.

The ocean breeze gently caressed his face, as if reassuring him that the journey ahead would be filled with wonders beyond imagination. The waves whispered promises of unity and harmony, carrying the echoes of his ancestors' wisdom. Hank felt a deep connection with the vast expanse before him, knowing that he was not alone in this grand undertaking.

With a heart filled with hope and a newfound understanding of his destiny, Hank looked out at the horizon, where the last rays of the sun painted the sky with breathtaking hues. The ocean stretched before him like an infinite canvas, inviting him to embark on a voyage that would forever change the course of his life.

As the stars began to twinkle in the night sky, Hank felt a sense of gratitude for his extraordinary journey, for the magical world that had revealed itself to him, and for the timeless wisdom of his ancestors that guided his path. With a sense of awe and wonder, he knew that the adventure had only just begun, and he was ready to dive deeper into the mysteries that awaited him in the heart of the ocean.

The End.

Book 2:
The Awakening of Dragons

"We don't have much time left," Kairos declared with urgency, his gaze encompassing the council members, as well as King Orion and Queen Seraphina, who stood in a solemn circle around the majestic Tree of Illumination. The weight of their mission hung heavy in the air.

His voice resonated with unwavering determination as he continued, "This unique convergence of the full moon and star alignments will soon shift. Our window to hold the portal through this celestial energy is rapidly closing. Since our last council meeting, we have prepared for this rare celestial alignment with planet Earth. It is the opportune moment to connect with the Doga and harness the immense power of the super full moon to bring Acacia back."

As Kairos's words lingered, a sudden disturbance shattered the fragile calm. In a fraction of a second, the moon was enshrouded in an unknown force, casting an ominous veil over the council members and obstructing their ability to channel the vital moonlight for the portal. The connection they had painstakingly established began to wane, leaving them bewildered and uncertain, and their collective gaze searching for answers in each other's eyes.

"It seems..." Lumina's voice faltered, her expression etched with deep concern, "...the dragon has been awakened."

To be continued.

Acknowledgements

Early this year, I spent a month in Egypt. Unlike my prior spiritual travels, this was my first solo trip there. Staying on Aswan's Heisa Island, where Philae Temple was only 15 minutes away, visiting Philae seemed like going to a grocery shop next door. I was far too spoiled being able to receive Goddess Isis, the Divine Mother's blessings anytime I wanted to. I'd slip on my flip-flops and sneak down to the Nile for a quick water purification ritual before entering the holy of holies, and then walk around the island until sunset when they closed the temple.

Over that month, thanks to the incredible synchronicities, I had the privilege and luxury of visiting the sanctuary of the temples in private and experiencing profound expansions and connections despite massive crowds in Egypt. I came to realize that the true refuge I had sought for years resided within me. Just like the cosmic diamond ray carried by Acacia, each of us holds the power to ignite the flame of the holy of holies in our own hearts.

"Fate, in its mysterious ways," as Grandma Titi said, guided me to an antique shop in Luxor during my last week in Egypt. There, I came across a ring with Thutmosis III's cartouche on it. After carefully selecting one from two exquisite designs and completing the purchase, fate took an unexpected turn when the shop owner accidentally broke the ring while wrapping it. With the swiftness of a seasoned seller, he cleverly and calmly responded, "Maybe this is a sign that you meant to bring the other ring." I paused. In that brief moment, the thought of an ancient curse, reminiscent of the mummy movies, crossed my mind. However, I trusted my guidance and accepted it.

For some reason, the ring seemed to boost my inspiration while writing this book as long as it rested on my finger. Once again, Egypt worked its magic on me with countless synchronicities and this serendipitous event.

Firstly, I offer my profound gratitude to the divine guidance that has graciously led me throughout the creation of this book, which has been beyond my imagination since I started.

At the core of my spiritual expedition lies the warm embrace of my soul family in Egypt: Emil Shaker, Hatem Aly, and Noha Aly. With their presence, I am always blessed and spoiled to enter the holy of holies at the exact time I need to be.

A heartfelt note of appreciation is especially reserved for Lala Chu and Dr. Black Bee. Despite their demanding daily workloads, they generously devoted their precious time to reviewing and refining my manuscript in Chinese and English. Their dedication breathed life into my story, and I am deeply grateful for their priceless contributions.

This book would be incomplete without all the stories and visions my psychic friends and spiritual companions shared during this wild ride. Their presence has enriched my path with diverse perspectives and profound insights, making this journey all the more magical.

To my beloved family members, and my cherished friends, I extend a tremendous thank you. Your loyal support has been the solid bedrock upon which I've built this incredible adventure. Even when my spiritual pursuits seemed unconventional or perplexing for the past 7 years after visiting Egypt and leaving my stable job, you stood by me with love and understanding. For that, I am always grateful.

About the Author

C.C. Adelaide is an Angelic Reiki master teacher and Akashic Record practitioner. Aside from writing and teaching, she also organizes holy site tours throughout the globe and crafts meditative scent products using herbs and resins she collects worldwide – her unique remedy of The Dreamy Dreamy.

"Quest for Acacia - The Cosmic Diamond Ray" is her first novel, in which she attempted to incorporate all the mystical and transcendent experiences she encountered at world sacred sites into a work of fantasy fiction.

Be among the first to receive notifications about upcoming releases, special promotions, and behind-the-scenes insights into C.C. Adelaide's creative process.

Scan QR Code to sign up.

Milton Keynes UK
Ingram Content Group UK Ltd.
UKHW041828241123
433237UK00002B/15